Welcome to the third of Rebecca Winters'
brand-new trilogy **LOVE UNDERCOVER**.

An award-winning author, Rebecca Winters writes
romances that pack an emotional punch you won't
forget! And her new miniseries is no exception.

Meet Annabelle, Gerard and Diana. Annabelle
and Gerard are private investigators, Diana, their
hardworking assistant. Each of them is about to
face a rather different assignment—falling in love!

Their mission was marriage!

Books in this series are:

MARCH #3545 UNDERCOVER FIANCÉE

APRIL #3549 UNDERCOVER BACHELOR

MAY #3553 UNDERCOVER BABY
Diana Rawlins had turned up at the hospital with
amnesia and a baby in her arms! She didn't remember
how either of them had happened. Her husband, Cal,
was determined to get to the bottom of the mystery—
especially as that seemed to be the only way he could
save his marriage!

Dear Reader,

Amnesia is a condition that has always fascinated me because it sets up so many possibilities for the person suffering from it, as well as the loved ones who must deal with it.

Recently I heard a story about a woman who lost her memory forever. As a result she divorced her husband. But this man loved her so much, he set out to win her love all over again. Six years later they were married.

I could only imagine the pain he went through, the rejection, the sacrifices he made, the challenges he faced because of his love for this woman. But as I imagined this, my own story, *Undercover Baby*, came to life. It's my personal tribute to this hero of a man who lived every word of the vows he made.

Happy reading,

Rebecca Winters

Undercover Baby
Rebecca Winters

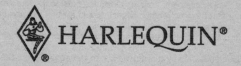

TORONTO • NEW YORK • LONDON
AMSTERDAM • PARIS • SYDNEY • HAMBURG
STOCKHOLM • ATHENS • TOKYO • MILAN • MADRID
PRAGUE • WARSAW • BUDAPEST • AUCKLAND

ISBN 0-373-03553-5

UNDERCOVER BABY

First North American Publication 1999.

This edition published by arrangement with Harlequin Books S.A.

® and TM are trademarks of the publisher. Trademarks indicated with ® are registered in the United States Patent and Trademark Office, the Canadian Trade Marks Office and in other countries.

Printed in U.S.A.

CHAPTER ONE

"Is THIS the Rawlins's residence?"

Cal Rawlins looped the bath towel around his neck, ready to put down the receiver in case it was a telemarketer. Seven-thirty in the morning was a little early to start listening to their unsolicited spiel.

If making love to his beautiful wife hadn't put him in such a good mood before he'd reluctantly let her out of bed on this beautiful June morning, he might have said he wasn't interested and then hung up.

"Yes, it is."

"This is the Bonneville Regional Hospital emergency room calling. Please don't be alarmed. The situation is not life threatening, but we have a Diana Rawlins here. Except for being disoriented from a fall, she appears to be all right. An initial examination reveals that the baby is jaundiced, but unharmed. A staff pediatrician has taken charge of his care. If you could come over—"

The mention of a baby filled Cal with unmitigated relief. "My wife's at work and we don't have any children." *Not yet anyway.* "I'm afraid you have the wrong Rawlins. Sorry."

He clicked off the phone and went back to the bathroom to finish shaving. His thoughts turned to their childless marriage, the only cloud threatening their happiness because she wanted to give him a baby so badly.

In the four years since their wedding, Diana had suffered three miscarriages, generally losing them at eight weeks. The last one had been devastating to both of them because she'd lost it after carrying it almost four months. A long enough time for them to decorate a nursery.

It had been a boy. They would have called him Tyler, after her grandfather.

When in future she conceived again, she would have to take it very easy and the doctor would perform a surgical procedure on the uterus to prevent the same problem from recurring. But so far, Diana hadn't conceived and she was frantic that she might never have a child.

Their obstetrician suggested that she was trying too hard, that she needed to relax and give her body a chance to rest before they tried to get pregnant again. Cal recognized the wisdom of the doctor's sound advice, but getting Diana to take it was a different story.

Cal had brought up the idea of adoption, but she'd adamantly refused to entertain it as a viable alternative. Still, he'd discussed the problem with Roman Lufka, Cal's best friend and Diana's boss at the LFK Associates International.

Both Roman and Cal agreed that if a baby were suddenly to become available, she might reconsider adoption. Oftentimes after obtaining a first child through legal means, a woman unexpectedly conceived. If time proved that Diana couldn't carry a baby full term, then the adoption idea was worth pursuing. Roman had his sources and said he would look into them.

Naturally Cal would have loved a baby of his own body and hers, but if that wasn't possible, then he welcomed the idea of adoption. Diana's happiness meant more to him than anything else. They had an exceptional marriage. He would do whatever it took to preserve the great love they shared. She was his life!

While Cal finished getting dressed for work, he decided to call his friend and suggest that they get together for lunch later in the day. Maybe Roman had new information on the subject.

His hand no sooner reached for the phone to call Roman than it rang again. When he picked up the receiver and said hello, he learned it was the hospital disturbing him for the second time. His brows formed a dark frown line.

"Mr. Rawlins? You *do* live at 18 Haxton Place here in Salt Lake?"

"Yes? But as I told you before, we don't have a baby."

"Nevertheless this woman says she's the baby's mother. We checked her driver's license. The address is listed as 18 Haxton Place, the same as yours." An odd chill passed through his body. "She's five feet six inches, long blond hair, green eyes, one hundred and twenty-four pounds."

Tightening his grip on the receiver he said, "That's my wife. Would it be possible to speak to her?"

"Not right now. As I told you a few minutes ago, the fall dazed her."

When did she fall? Where?

"I'll be right there."

Feeling like he'd been kicked in the gut, he raced out of the house. Disobeying the speed limit, he drove his Saab to the hospital in record time.

He swallowed hard when he spotted her white

Buick parked halfway up the block. Its presence confirmed that she had indeed driven to the hospital earlier that morning. She'd only been gone from the house a little more than an hour.

What in the hell had happened in that amount of time? The mention of a baby made no sense at all.

"I'm Mr. Rawlins," he said the second he reached the admission desk outside the emergency room doors. "I'd like to see my wife, Diana."

"Take a seat over there and someone will be right with you."

With his adrenaline pumping, Cal preferred to remain standing. He would just as soon not have to look at all the anxious people who filled the reception area.

Thankfully the person who'd called the house had reassured him Diana's condition wasn't serious.

"Mr. Rawlins? I'm Dr. Farr, the one who first examined your wife. Come on in here and we'll talk."

Relieved to get some answers at last, Cal followed the short, wiry doctor through another set of doors to an empty examination room. He thought of course the other man would take him straight to Diana. The fact that he didn't, served to deepen the pit in Cal's stomach.

"Is my wife all right? That's all I want to know."

Dr. Farr looked up at Cal. "When she fell, she hit the back of her head hard enough to break the skin and form a small lump. The X ray didn't reveal anything abnormal, but her concussion has left her disoriented. I've asked Dr. Harkness, a neurosurgeon on staff at the hospital, to come down and examine her. He should be here shortly."

When the significance of his words sank in, Cal's head reared back. "How bad is her disorientation?"

The other man eyed Cal compassionately. "A couple of ambulance attendants found her outside the emergency room entrance. She was sitting on the pavement in a dazed condition, clutching her baby.

"She couldn't remember her name, where she lived, or what she was doing there. They had to look inside her purse for identification so they could call you."

Good Lord.

Cal's body broke out in a cold sweat. "Did someone see her fall? How do you know she wasn't attacked?"

"We assume she slipped on the cement. The path is on an incline, so she probably fell backward. There was blood where her head hit, and the backs of her elbows are skinned. The baby didn't appear to suffer any injury, but as you were told earlier, his bilirubin count is too high. To treat him for the jaundice, the pediatrician has put him under the lights."

Cal shook his head in disbelief. "I have no idea whose baby it is."

"A friend's perhaps?"

"Possibly, though I can't think of anyone close to us. Maybe Diana offered to baby-sit someone's child and forgot to tell me. But I don't see how that could be when she was on her way to work."

"Well, it shouldn't be too long before your wife starts to recall what happened."

"I hope you're right. Can I see her now?"

"Of course. Come with me. Please don't be unduly concerned by her condition, Mr. Rawlins. Memory loss is a fairly common occurrence with some head injury patients."

Memory loss was another word for amnesia. Just the word made Cal cringe.

"In the majority of cases, it's temporary. She'll probably be back to her normal self within twelve hours or so. I just wanted you to be prepared in case you went in to see her and she didn't recognize you right away."

Not recognize me?

Cal scoffed at the notion. She might be dazed, but there was no way in this world she wouldn't know her own husband. They'd been soul mates from the moment they'd met.

Your soul could never forget an integral part of itself, he reasoned inwardly.

"She's right in there. When you need to talk to me, I'll be at the front desk."

Nodding to the doctor Cal headed for the cubicle, his heart revving like a race engine. As he stepped inside the curtain, he couldn't wait to embrace his wife who'd only been gone from his arms a short while.

He found Diana lying on her right side, facing him. From this angle he couldn't tell that she'd sustained an injury to the back of her head.

Instead of the leaf-green shirtwaist dress which had molded her gorgeous figure earlier, she was wearing a hospital gown and appeared to be asleep. Her shoulder-length hair fanned out on the pillow, exactly as she'd worn it when she'd gotten ready for work.

Except for the smudges beneath her eyes where the dark lashes rested against her pale cheeks, she looked vulnerable as hell, but perfectly normal to him. *Thank God.*

Hopefully he'd be able to take her home within the next couple of hours.

One arm lay on top of the sheet covering her body. He leaned over to examine her elbow with his fingertip. The skin around the bandage showed definite signs of having been scraped. At the slight contact, her lips made an unfamiliar moue, then her eyelids fluttered open.

"Diana?" he cried in relief to see she was awake. In an instinctive move, he covered her mouth with his own, needing a repeat demonstration of the physical love they'd shared that morning before she'd left the house.

When she wouldn't allow him to deepen their kiss, he tried gently to coax her lips apart to provoke the response he craved.

"No—" she begged in alarm. "Please don't." She pushed her free hand against his shoulder.

Never once in their lives had she rejected him. Bewildered by her behavior, he raised his head to look down at her. The green eyes staring back at him showed no sign of recognition. Only anxiety.

Lord.

She really doesn't know who I am.

That's impossible!

"Diana, it's me, Cal. Your husband. For the love of God, darling— Say something!"

He waited for her to cry out the words he needed to hear.

"I'm sorry," she finally whispered, "but I have no idea who you are. Can I please talk to the doctor?"

Terror seized Cal's heart so that he was slow to hear her plea.

The tall, broad-shouldered stranger at her bedside

had just announced he was her husband, Cal. He'd called her Diana, and he'd kissed her with the ease of longtime familiarity.

Since she'd been brought in to emergency, Dr. Farr had referred to her as Mrs. Rawlins. Apparently she had no family other than her husband who would be arriving at the hospital shortly.

She studied the man whose brown hair matched the color of his pain-filled eyes. He reminded her of those men on horseback she'd seen in magazine ads depicting the West, rugged individualists with hard-boned faces and chiseled features. Yet this man was dressed in a light brown business suit and tie, cloaking him in a mantle of urbane sophistication.

He looked successful, confident. Very much a master of his own destiny. She couldn't imagine being married to someone who appeared so dominant and male.

Perspiration leaked from every pore of her body. She moaned in panic because she was unable to recall anything before they'd brought her and the baby into the emergency room.

The torment coming from the stranger's eyes made her feel uncomfortable, *and guilty,* because she couldn't do anything to alleviate it.

Her gaze slid away to focus on the large, breathtaking diamond of her engagement ring. It, plus a wide gold wedding band on the ring finger of her left hand, attested to the fact that she'd been through the process of an engagement and marriage to him. They'd had a child together.

The baby!

Right now she needed Tyler desperately.

Why hadn't someone brought him back to her yet?

The emergency room doctor had assured her that her little boy was all right, so what could be taking so long?

Wishing the man who claimed to be her husband would go away, she asked, "Could you do me a favor, please?"

"You know I'd do anything for you, darling," came his husky response at last. "What is it?"

He'd been hovering over her. Combined with his loving attitude, she felt smothered and wished he would go away. "Would you please find Tyler and bring him to me?"

"Tyler?"

"My baby!" she blurted, not understanding why his voice had sounded so strange just now. But the strain of trying to get through to him had started up the horrible throbbing at the back of her skull once more. Nausea washed over her in waves.

"I just want Tyler," she half sobbed. Tears poured down her cheeks. "They said he wasn't injured in the fall, but maybe the pediatrician has found something wrong after all."

His lips brushed her moist cheek. "I'll be right back, my love."

After he left the room, she breathed more easily. If he touched her again or used more any more endearments, she would ask the nurse to tell him to stay away.

Hurt because she'd winced when he'd kissed her, Cal wheeled out of the cubicle and made a beeline for Dr. Farr who was filling out a chart. At his approach, the doctor looked up.

"How is your wife? Did she recognize you?"

"Not yet." He expelled the breath he'd been holding. "But she referred to the baby as Tyler, which is a step in the right direction." Cal then proceeded to explain the significance of the name.

The other man gave him an encouraging smile. "No doubt about it. Her memory is returning. I'm sure Dr. Harkness will agree. Too bad something has held him up. I'll make another inquiry and send him to you as soon as he comes into emergency."

"I would appreciate that. However, there's another problem. Diana's worried about the baby and wants to see him to make sure he's all right. After what I've told you about her last miscarriage, I don't think it's a good idea."

"I understand where you're coming from, Mr. Rawlins. You don't want her to get unduly attached to a baby that isn't hers. On the other hand, I'd like to decrease any anxiety she's feeling right now. If seeing the baby will bring her momentary comfort, that might be the best medicine to hasten the initial healing process."

In his heart of hearts Cal knew that for the time being, the baby was the only thing that would console his wife. The fact that she didn't need or want him, *her own husband,* cut deeper than a knife. But he realized he had to put her desires ahead of his own.

"How old is the infant?"

"I estimate three, maybe four days."

So young!

A shudder passed through Cal's body. His wife would find a virtual newborn irresistible.

Diana, darling— Where did the baby come from? What were you doing with it? Lord, what a nightmare.

"Could you ask someone to bring the baby down to her?"

"It could be under the lights for a while. But I'll find out what I can and keep you posted. In the meantime, go back to your wife and see if your conversation jars her memory a little more."

He nodded. But first he needed to get hold of Roman.

Someone's baby was missing.

If Diana couldn't shed any light on the situation within the next little while, this could become a police matter. Roman would know exactly how to handle it and be discreet at the same time.

Cal didn't think for a minute that his wife had gone off the deep end, and had stolen the baby. But whatever the explanation, when she regained her full memory she would be loathe to give it up.

This accident had happened too soon after her last miscarriage. More than ever he felt it vital to go ahead and start adoption proceedings.

Needing privacy, he found the empty examination room and called his friend on his cellular phone.

"Roman, here."

"Roman? It's Cal."

"Hey! I'm glad you called. I was just telling Brittany the four of us need to get together this weekend. By the way, where's the best assistant I've ever had? She told me she was going to come in early to catch up on some paperwork."

"That's what I'm calling about. *Lord, Roman.* I'm at Bonneville Regional. Diana's in the emergency room with a head injury."

"What?"

Cal's eyes closed tightly. He was too broken up to talk.

"Say no more. I'll be right there."

"Thanks,'" Cal said in a hoarse whisper, and put the phone back in his pocket. Right now he needed his buddy to help make sense of this nightmare. *"Thank God for Roman,"* he murmured, hurrying to Diana's cubicle.

By this time another doctor was examining her, asking her questions. Cal figured it was Dr. Harkness. With eye signals the neurosurgeon indicated he wanted to be alone with his patient and would talk to Cal later.

He fought the desire to inform the doctor that he was Diana's husband, that he wanted to be involved. However Dr. Harkness had left him with no choice but to return to the reception area.

Since the examination might take some time, Cal decided to go outside and wait for Roman. He needed to fill his lungs with fresh air that wasn't tainted by the smell of antiseptic. On the way out, he asked someone to show him where his wife had fallen.

One of the ambulance attendants accompanied him to the spot, but any sign of an accident had been cleaned up.

"Did anyone see her fall?"

"Not that I know of, sir. We went out when an ambulance drove in and noticed her sitting on the path. Her pupils were dilated. She couldn't tell us any information, so we brought her inside."

"Okay. Thanks."

Without wasting another second he strode swiftly toward her parked car. She'd left the doors unlocked, something she normally never did for safety reasons.

It meant she was in such a hurry to get inside the emergency room, she didn't bother.

Suddenly his eye caught sight of a rectangular carton in the back seat. It was the kind of box that held produce meant for a grocery store. With a jerk, he opened the back door and reached for the box. The empty carton had been lined with a thin, wrinkled cotton blanket.

Dear Lord. Had she found the baby in this box?

"Cal?" a familiar male voice called out.

Cal whirled around to see Roman standing there. He must have flown from his office to make it here this fast.

"What's going on?"

After emitting a tortured sigh, Cal told his friend everything he knew. "The hell of it is, she didn't recognize me, Roman."

He felt a clap on his shoulder. "When I was on the police force, I investigated a lot of accidents and saw plenty of cases like this. Her amnesia is temporary."

Cal shivered again. "You can't imagine what it's like to kiss your wife, look into her eyes, only to see fear and repulsion there."

"No, I can't. But she only fell a couple of hours ago. Give it time for her mind and body to absorb the shock. It won't be long before she's back to normal. Meanwhile, let's see if there's anything else in the car that will give us a clue as to what happened."

Roman's was the voice of sanity. Together they searched the immaculate interior, but found nothing else.

"Have you looked in her purse or her clothes?"

"No," Cal answered in a hoarse voice. "Her reaction to me left me too shaken up to think, period."

"I hear you. Let's go inside the hospital and see if we can find anything else that will shed some light."

Cal nodded before the two of them went back to the emergency room. Dr. Harkness met them at the desk.

After exchanging the amenities he said, "I concur with the attending physician's diagnosis. She's suffering the kind of amnesia brought on by head trauma.

"There's been no loss of knowledge of the things around her. For example, she knows she's in a hospital, she can tell time, add numbers, all of those details. But for now she has blocked out past events. In time, she'll recover her memory."

"How soon, Doctor?"

"No one has the answer to that question. You just have to be patient. My advice is to feed her information on a need-to-know basis only. Her mind is refusing to let her remember, possibly because she doesn't want to remember." One blond brow lifted. "Has something happened recently that has been very painful for her?"

Cal started to nod. "She's had three miscarriages in a row. The most recent one dealt us both a severe blow. Since then, Diana has been obsessed by the idea that she might not be able to conceive again, let alone have a child. She's wanted a baby ever since we were married."

"That could explain the reason why it might take longer for her to get her memory back, Mr. Rawlins. Dr. Farr tells me the baby she was holding isn't yours, that you have no idea whose it is."

"None at all. Roman, here, is the head of the Lufka detective agency. He's going to start an investigation to find out whose baby it is, and why Diana happened to have the baby with her.''

The doctor's expression sobered. "That's good. But as you've realized by now, she believes the baby is hers.''

"Yes. That's what's got me worried.''

"I confess I don't like it, either. Dr. Farr told me you would rather she didn't see the baby again. I tend to agree with you, yet I also feel that the other doctor has a point. The baby would be good for her right now to comfort her in her fear. She's very frightened that she can't remember anything about her life with you. She's clinging to that child because she needs something to love that is familiar to her.''

"What should I do?''

"For the time being, the baby has jaundice and can't be moved from the lights until the pediatrician gives the go ahead. I've told your wife about his condition. She seems to have accepted the fact that she'll have to wait until he's improved before she's allowed to see him.

"Thankfully the baby's condition, which is not life threatening now that he's being given the proper care, has bought us some time. We can hope that as you stay with your wife, keep her company and anticipate her needs, she'll start to remember things on her own. The memory usually comes back in bits and pieces with little effort.''

"Except that she's repulsed by my presence,'' Cal ground out.

"She told me she's afraid of you. That's why I didn't invite you to stay for the examination. It's a natural reaction. She has to go on blind faith that you are her husband, that you two love each other and have been happily married. To her, you're a complete stranger.

"I'm going to have her admitted overnight for observation. In the morning, if all her vital signs are stable, and another X-ray doesn't show any problems, I'll let you take her home.

"For the time being, my advice for what it's worth is to treat her like a sister rather than a wife. Slowly but surely allow friends and relatives to come around, but warn them not to upset her or act startled by her loss of memory. Always be supportive, friendly, tender, kind. Don't overreact when she retreats. She's only protecting herself. Don't make physical advances."

Cal shook his head. "I already did when I kissed her and she didn't kiss me back." The pain of her rejection had gone soul deep.

"A perfectly natural gesture on your part, but it explains her anxiety. Until her memory returns, she has to regain her trust of you. I'm afraid the burden is on your shoulders, Mr. Rawlins. However I want to assure you that I believe her condition is temporary. In time you'll have her back as good as new."

He turned to Roman. "We've had to report Baby Doe to the police, but perhaps your investigation will produce swifter results. Let us know, will you?"

"Of course. I'm hoping to have answers within a few hours."

"Good. Then I'll talk to both of you later. The hospital will keep me notified if there are changes in your wife's condition. If you have any concerns at all, feel free to ask someone at the desk to phone me."

"Thank you, Dr. Harkness."

He smiled. "She's a lovely woman. I can understand your fear. This is the time when the wedding vows start to take on a whole new meaning."

Cal pondered the doctor's words. He knew the other man was trying to commiserate, but could anyone understand a situation like this unless they had experienced it for themselves?

"You all right, Cal?"

The concern in Roman's voice jerked him back to the present.

"No, but I'm going to *have* to be, aren't I?"

The rhetorical question required no response. Roman shifted his weight. "After listening to Dr. Harkness, I think it would be better if I don't see Diana until tomorrow or even the next day. One person at a time. It makes sense to me.

"What I want you to do is ask an attendant to bring her belongings out here. Tell them to make up any excuse they want so they won't alarm her unduly. I might find a clue. It's the first place I need to start. Then I'm going back to the office. Maybe she left some kind of clue there which I didn't see at the time.

"We know she was on her way to work this morning and made no mention of tending anyone's baby. So it's my guess the baby was either placed in her car or—"

"Or placed on the doorstep at work!" Cal blurted. "If it had been on our doorstep or in our car when she left the garage, she would have run in the house to tell me."

"Unless it was still kind of dark and she didn't notice it on the back seat until she got to work."

"That's a possibility, except that she almost always

locks the car doors. Someone would have had to force entry to even get in the garage."

"Whatever, following this to its logical conclusion, if the baby looked yellow to her, she might have been so concerned, she didn't think to call anyone. Instead she felt it was an emergency and immediately drove to the hospital figuring an ambulance couldn't get there any faster. Obviously in her haste, she slipped and fell."

"That's it, Roman! That *has* to be the explanation."

"As soon as you can, get me her things, and I mean *everything,* we should have answers before long."

"I owe you for this, Roman."

"Then we're more than even. I can't count the times you've come to my rescue, especially when I was working on Brittany's case. You and Diana helped me keep my sanity before I made her my wife. Now it's my turn to help you. I've never made it any secret that I love Diana. So do the other PI's. She's the best thing that ever happened to the agency. When the guys hear what happened, it's going to come as a horrible shock, particularly to Brittany and Annabelle."

"I know. Those three have grown as close as sisters."

"I'll inform everybody. You go back to Diana and let us handle the investigation."

Cal put a hand on Roman's shoulder. "Wait here just a minute. I'll get someone to bring out her things." He found an attendant nearby and told her what they needed from Diana's cubicle.

"No problem. The doctor has just given orders to take her up to a private room on the fourth floor, 418

North. I'll just tell her we're going to load her stuff on a cart first.''

''Perfect.''

In short order the attendant came back with a large sack provided by the hospital containing Diana's personal effects. Cal handed it over to Roman. ''I hope you find something. For Diana's own good, the sooner the mystery about the baby is cleared up, the better.''

''Don't worry. We'll be fast and thorough. I'm going out to her car for the box and blanket. One of the guys will be by later to drive the car back to your house. In the meantime, as soon as I discover anything, I'll phone you on your cellular.''

Cal nodded. He couldn't ask for more than that. Right now as he stared at Roman's departing back, he realized his friend's level-headed thinking was the only thing keeping him from going right over the edge.

CHAPTER TWO

"Nurse?"

"Yes, Mrs. Rawlins?"

"Could you call me Diana, please?"

"Of course. If you'll call me Jane."

"All right. Jane? I overheard Dr. Farr say my baby is four days old. I don't understand why I'm not sore and bleeding after my delivery. Why hasn't my milk come in yet?"

"That's something to ask the doctor when he makes his rounds this evening. Don't worry. The baby is being well taken care of in the nursery."

"How soon can I see him?"

"He needs to stay under the lights until tomorrow, at least."

"Then will you help me to go to the nursery so I can sit with him?"

"That's against doctor's orders, Diana. We've just settled you in your room. He left strict instructions for you to have rest and stay quiet. You want to get better, don't you?

"Your husband has gone home to bring you some of your things. When he returns, you can talk to him about it. But if you can wait until this evening, Dr. Harkness will make his rounds. Perhaps he'll allow you and your husband to go to the nursery for a peek. Everything depends on how you and the baby are feeling by then."

"You don't understand, Jane. I don't remember him being my husband— All I want is my baby!"

"I know. But you want him to get better, too, don't you?"

"Of course."

"Then try to be patient. I know it's hard. After that nasty fall, you need to give yourself a chance to heal. I'd also like to see that temperature go down. Tell you what. I'll look in on you again in a little while."

"Don't go!"

The nurse walked over to the side of the bed. "What's frightening you the most?"

Diana hid her face in her hands. "I don't know. *Everything*."

"Of course it is. If I couldn't remember anything of my past life, I'd be frightened, too. But this is a temporary situation. You remember having the baby with you when you fell. That means your memory is returning. Just give it a little more time."

She lifted her tear-drenched face. "That's true, isn't it? I remembered his name was Tyler."

"That's right. And you'll start remembering more and more."

"But that's just it! I don't remember anything else. Mr. Rawlins acts so hurt around me, I can hardly bear it."

"Naturally he has been affected by your fall. He says everything was wonderful between you when you left for work this morning, and then he gets a call saying that you're in the hospital and can't remember what happened."

"My work?" she blurted, scarcely listening to anything else. *What kind of work?*

This was another revelation she couldn't fathom

because she had no memory of it. Why would she be going to work when she'd just had a baby?

"That's what I understand," Jane informed her, "but I'll leave that to your husband to explain. He should be back soon. I must say he loves you very much. It's obvious to the staff that he would do anything for you."

"I don't want his solicitation."

"Maybe not, but if you could put yourself in his place for a moment, you would understand that he is as frightened as you are."

"What does he have to be frightened about? He *knows* me."

"That's true, but he's married to a woman who doesn't know *him*. You're treating him like you would anyone off the street because you can't do anything else. How do you suppose you would feel if your positions were reversed and he wanted nothing to do with you?"

Diana bit her lip and turned her head toward the wall. The movement hurt the spot on the back of her head where they'd bandaged it. She didn't like Jane reminding her that Cal Rawlins was in pain.

"If you want company, I'll send one of the volunteers down to read to you or whatever you'd like."

"No. I think I want to be alone now."

"I'll check on another couple of patients, then come back."

"Thank you." She fought more tears. "I'm sorry I'm behaving so abominably."

"The fact that you can apologize for something that is beyond your control tells me that at heart you're a very kind, sensitive woman who wouldn't purposely hurt anyone."

But am I? How does Jane know that?

When the door was shut, Diana reached under the bedsheet to feel her stomach. It was flat and smooth as silk. There were no pads covering a sore incision, which meant she hadn't had a Cesarean section.

While she lay there, it came to her that she hadn't given birth to her baby. She couldn't have, or there would be all the normal signs!

Had she adopted it?

Nobody had said a word about anything.

Dear God. What was really going on?

For the first time since coming into the hospital, she was anxious to talk to Mr. Rawlins. He appeared to be the only person who could give her the answers she needed.

But would he be honest with her? How could she trust a perfect stranger?

Cal had barely entered his house to pack a bag for Diana when his cellular phone rang. He reached in his pocket and put it to his ear.

"Roman? I saw your name on the Caller ID."

"I told you I'd touch base when I had something. You and I were right on."

He gripped the phone tighter. "Go ahead. I'm listening."

"I found a note tucked in the pocket of Diana's dress, the one folded in the hospital bag. The paper has been ripped from a steno pad. The typed message reads,

"*Dear Diana,*
My boyfriend and I talked it over and decided we had to give up the baby because we can't take care

of it. A friend told me about you and how much you've been wanting one, so I brought him to your work. She says that you and your husband are the nicest people in the world, and that you would make the perfect parents. She also said you have a nursery all ready for a baby boy, and I want my boy to have the best of everything, so I'm giving him to you and nobody else. I've asked God if I'm doing the right thing and I feel really good inside about this. Please take care of him and love him. I wish we could, but we can't. I'll ask one more favor. Please take him to church so he can learn about God. I always liked church and I know that if you do that for him, the three of you will have a perfect life. Thank you very much. And one more favor. When he gets older, tell him we loved him too much to try and keep him."

The simplicity, the poignancy, of the young mother's words caused tears to prick Cal's eyes. She loved her baby. It took amazing faith and courage to do what she did. What a hell of a situation. That note must have wrung Diana's heart.

"*Lord, Roman.* This is incredible."

"You can say that again. No doubt Diana's compassionate instincts took right over. One look at the sick baby and she rushed him to the emergency room for treatment."

Cal's mind was leaping ahead. "If Diana were to read that note, it might help bring her memory back faster."

"I agree. Before I can give it to you, I have to contact the police and let them know what we've learned. That note exonerates Diana from any wrong-doing and will be used as evidence.''

Roman had been reading Cal's mind. Neither man had wanted to say anything earlier, but both knew the circumstances of Diana suddenly claiming a newborn as her own would look suspicious in the eyes of the law, regardless of her head injury.

Filled with relief that at least this much of the mystery was solved, Cal could concentrate fully on Diana. ''I'm going back to the hospital in a few minutes and I'll let them know what we've learned.''

''Good. In the meantime I'll get started tracking down this young mother. She's given us plenty of information, but I'm not so sure her boyfriend had anything to do with her decision. I wouldn't be surprised if he disappeared on her a long time ago and she's trying to save face. Nevertheless she's friendly with someone who has a connection with the agency, otherwise she couldn't have known about Diana and her desire for a baby.

''The girl is probably in her midteens. She may not have gone to a hospital for her delivery, but on the chance that she did, I'll run a check on all the babies delivered within the last week. I'd like to find her. There are programs to help unwed mothers keep their babies.''

''What if she doesn't turn up?''

''Then the baby will become a ward of the court and placed in foster care until it's adopted.''

Adopted.

''What if—''

''I'm way ahead of you Cal. That's why I want to conduct a thorough search for the baby's mother. Some mothers regret their decision and come back for their babies, or cause trouble later on down the road.

"In this case the mother knows exactly where to come. The last thing an adoptive couple would want or need is to have the birth mother show up after the legal proceedings were concluded. But we're getting way ahead of ourselves here, and I can't guarantee anything."

"I realize that. But if anyone can do the impossible, it's you. Roman?" Cal's voice was gruff with emotion. "I can't thank you enough for being there."

"Save it. Get back to your wife. We'll stay in touch."

"Right."

A few minutes later Cal drove to the hospital with some clothes and personal articles for Diana, including their wedding photo album and another scrapbook. Hoping to jog her memory, he also brought the novel she'd been reading. When he saw that the mail had been delivered, he took that along, too, bills and all. The latest issue of *Detective Inc,* had come. She always went for that magazine first because she wanted to keep up to date and be the best assistant possible to Roman.

Enroute to the hospital Cal made another call to his private secretary, Mrs. West. After updating her on Diana's condition, he informed her that he would be out of the office for several days. If something came up she couldn't handle, she could reach him on his cellular.

With that taken care of, he pulled into the car park and dashed inside the hospital, praying that Diana had started to remember something else besides the baby. *That she remembered him.*

His first instinct was to open the door to her room and go in unannounced. But the doctor had cautioned him to treat her like a sister, so he knocked.

"Yes?"

"Diana? It's Cal. Is it all right if I come in?"

"Give me a minute, please."

The old Diana wouldn't have needed a knock. She would never have kept him waiting. His Diana of six hours ago would have welcomed him with open arms, no matter her condition.

His jaw hardened because he realized the miracle he'd been waiting for hadn't happened yet.

"Of course. Take all the time you need."

It seemed an eternity before she said, "You can come in now."

Cal entered her room and closed the door behind him. He felt like an intruder.

Dear God. She was his wife. How was he going to handle being around her and not touching her, holding her?

He still couldn't fathom that any of this had happened—that she was sitting primly in the hospital bed, the covers up to her chin, looking fragile and so damn nervous of him he felt like someone had just slugged him in the midsection.

"I brought you several changes of clothes and a few things to read."

Her meek little thank-you sparked another surge of adrenaline. When she didn't extend her hands, he left the things he'd brought on her bedside table.

Needing to channel his negative energy, he hung up a couple of items in the closet, then put the rest of her clothes away in the drawers.

"How are you feeling now?" he asked, pulling up a chair to the side of her bed.

"I still don't remember anything, if that's what you're asking." She said this with her head lowered. He had the idea she couldn't stand to look at him. "I'm sorry if that brings you pain."

Her blunt speaking took his breath. Diana had always been an honest person, but normally she was more gentle in her approach. The doctor had told him to treat her like a family member, but he'd never had a sister or brother and couldn't pretend something he didn't feel. He had a premonition that under these precarious circumstances, finding common ground would prove virtually impossible. There were no guidelines. He would have to feel his way.

"I could lie and say I was only inquiring about the physical pain to the back of your head. The truth is, I'm shattered by what has happened to you, to me. To *us.* Any way you look at it, this is a hellish situation. If we're not totally honest with each other, then I don't see how we'll be able to work our way out of this nightmare. I realize you're terrified of me."

That brought her head up. She stared at him. Again, he could see his presence didn't register with her except to upset her.

"I am, but not because you're a terrifying person. I'm sure you're probably a wonderful person," she admitted in a quiet voice. "But I don't know you. I have no feeling for you. That's what is terrifying."

Oh, Lord.

"I'm beginning to realize that. Just give me some time to deal with it."

"Of course." He heard a troubled sigh escape.

"The only thing real to me is the baby. Obviously I didn't give birth to him."

He blinked in surprise. "Who told you that?"

"Why would I have to be told something that is vastly apparent? I overheard the doctor say that the baby is only four days old, and I show no signs of ever having been pregnant. Which means we adopted him. Couldn't I have children, or was it a physical problem on your part?"

Give your wife information on a need-to-know basis.

Unable to remain seated, he got up and wandered over to the window which looked out on the foothills of the city. *Was this one of those moments?*

"Why aren't you saying anything? Is it because before the accident, I couldn't handle the fact that I wasn't able to conceive, or something like that, and you're afraid to bring it up to me now?"

Diana, Diana...

"Since I have no idea of how I used to be, it really doesn't matter, does it?"

It did once, my darling. You wouldn't even discuss the possibility of adoption.

"I thought you were going to be honest with me."

"I want to be." His voice grated.

"So why the hesitation?"

He rubbed the back of his neck before turning from the window to look at her. "Because I don't want to upset you. What I'm about to tell you could do just that. I would rather have waited for your memory to return, then no explanation would be necessary."

She laced her hands together nervously. "But we don't know when that day will come. *If ever.*"

"Don't say that!" Her words filled him with fresh anguish.

"I have to. Some people lose their memories and never regain them."

Dear God. You can remember everything about life except your own life! It doesn't make any sense.

"Dr. Harkness says your memory will return." Cal had to believe that or lose his mind.

"Maybe. In the meantime, do you expect me to live in a vacuum?" she blurted. "I'd rather be dead."

Cal groaned. "Never talk that way again, Diana. Not even in jest."

"You're not inside my skin."

My wife— Where have you gone? I don't know you like this.

He swallowed hard. "No. I'm not. I couldn't begin to understand how you feel."

"Thank you for saying that." Her voice wobbled.

He wanted to wrap her in his arms and will her memory back, but he couldn't do anything. *Not one damn thing.* He'd never felt so helpless in his life.

"Please—if you care for me at all, tell me the truth."

"All right." He placed his hands on the back of the chair. "That baby upstairs is not our baby."

"What? But of course it is! It's Tyler!"

"No, Diana. You say you want to hear the truth, but already you're fighting me."

An awkward silence prevailed. "D-did we fight a lot in our marriage?"

He swallowed hard. "Never."

After a long silence she whispered, "I'm sorry. Please go on."

His heart reacted like a runaway train. "I don't

know if this is a good idea. Why don't we wait for the doctor?''

She shook her head. ''Don't do this to me. Finish telling me the truth. I have to hear it. I promise I won't interrupt again.''

I'm damned whatever I do, aren't I, sweetheart?

''We're pretty sure you found him on the doorstep at your work this morning. He was lying in a grocery box. There was a note. The unwed mother who left the baby there knew you would discover him. When you saw that the baby was jaundiced, you immediately brought him to the hospital for care.

''On your way into the emergency room, you slipped and hit your head on the pavement. Some ambulance attendants found you sitting on the cement, holding him. That's why they brought you inside. When you couldn't remember anything, they looked in your purse, found your identification and called me.''

Her lustrous green eyes filled with tears. ''Tyler's really not my baby,'' she murmured in agony.

What have I said, what have I done?

Go on, Rawlins. Finish it.

''No. An abandoned baby is a ward of the court. You called him Tyler because that was your grandfather's name. It's the name you had hoped to call our baby, the one you miscarried a few months ago.''

''I had a miscarriage?''

He nodded. ''You've had three, the last one after you were four months along,'' he said gently.

''*No!*'' Her look of horror mixed with a hint of pleading tore him apart.

''You asked for the truth. I didn't want to hurt you. God knows I didn't.''

Tears gushed from her eyes, forming rivulets down her pale cheeks. Suddenly she was convulsed. Her despair was worse than anything he'd heard during the traumatic week following her last miscarriage when she'd cried nonstop for days.

"Darli—"

"Don't call me that!" she broke in on him. "For the love of heaven. Just go away and leave me alone."

Sick in a way he couldn't describe, Cal left her bedside and headed out of the room for the nursing station. The nurse who'd settled Diana in was just coming down the hall.

"What's wrong, Mr. Rawlins? You look ill."

Cal groaned in response. He ran a shaky hand through his hair. Clearing his throat he said, "Diana figured out she didn't give birth to the baby upstairs in the nursery, so she forced me to tell her the truth. Now she's inconsolable and it's my fault." His voice shook. "My wife needs help!"

The nurse eyed him with compassion. "I know this is hard on you. While I call Dr. Harkness, why don't you take a seat in the waiting room around the corner. I'll find you as soon as I've talked to him."

Cal nodded.

Like the shell-shocked victim of a bombing, he made his way to the lounge, trying to grasp the enormity of what had happened since his wife had left his bed earlier that morning.

"Cal?"

At the sound of a familiar female voice he turned in time to see Annabelle—one of their best friends, and a crack member of Roman's PI team—come rushing toward him.

"Roman just told me what happened. I got here as soon as I could."

Little as she was, her physical and emotional support was exactly what he needed right now. They reached for each other. The contact caused him to break down. In a rush of emotion everything spilled out, particularly his fears.

"Diana not only sees me as a stranger, Annie, she *despises* me. What if she never regains her memory? What if she has gone away from me forever?"

"Don't think like that," she urged him. "Roman told me the doctor said her condition was temporary."

Cal grimaced. "But what if he's wrong? I don't know why, but I have this gut instinct she's never going to remember me or our marriage."

Annabelle's arms tightened. "You're getting way ahead of yourself. But if—and I say that's a huge if— the day should come that you discover her amnesia is permanent, then I know you'll find a way to make her fall in love with you all over again."

Her words seeped into his soul.

If Diana's amnesia is permanent, I know you'll find a way to make her fall in love with you all over again.

Haunted by such a daunting prospect, he shook his head. "If you had heard the enmity in her voice when she told me to get out of her room a few minutes ago, you wouldn't be saying that to me now."

Annabelle let go of him and lifted her head, giving him a direct stare. "It's too soon to talk about the *what-ifs,* Cal. Give it a few days. She has withstood a severe head trauma. The pain must be pretty bad.

Naturally she's not herself. Whatever she says or does right now, don't take it personally.''

"How can I not? The doctor says that if there are no complications, she can be released from the hospital tomorrow. What if she refuses to go home with me?''

"No one can answer that question yet. Let's wait and see what he has to say about her condition the next time he examines her. As for you, you're coming to our house tonight. Rand told me to tell you that's an order.''

"Thanks, Annie. I appreciate that, but I couldn't go anywhere. I'm staying here in case she remembers something and needs me.''

"Then we'll keep the vigil with you.''

"I couldn't ask you to do that.''

"You didn't ask. I'm offering. Don't forget. My husband and I love Diana, too. Wait here while I go say hello to her. Maybe she'll refuse to talk to me, maybe she won't. But since you were honest with her about the baby, then there are no secrets and I won't have to tiptoe around her. I think it's important that she knows she has friends she can count on, even if we are strangers to her.''

"I agree. Thanks, Annie,'' he whispered.

She raised up to kiss his cheek. "No thanks necessary. I won't be long. In the meantime, sit down and drink this.'' She put some change in the pop machine and handed him a cola. "You probably didn't eat breakfast.''

"No.''

"Rand will be here shortly. I'll ask him to bring food for all of us.''

Like Roman, Annabelle kept a level head under

stress, providing temporary calm to Cal's tortured thoughts. He found himself praying that her appearance might trigger the mechanism that propelled Diana back to the world the rest of them inhabited. But deep inside, a part of him still feared her condition was irreversible.

How was he going to live with that?

CHAPTER THREE

"DIANA? It's Annabelle Dunbarton. I know you don't know me from Adam, but before the accident we were best friends. May I come in for a minute?"

Diana was lying on her stomach, her face buried in the pillow where she'd been sobbing. At the sound of the stranger's voice she felt relief that it wasn't Cal Rawlins. Just minutes earlier Jane had promised to keep him away until after the doctor had come down to examine her again.

Dr. Harkness couldn't arrive soon enough for her. She didn't care if the baby wasn't hers. She wanted to go up to the nursery and see him. In order to do that, she would need the doctor's permission.

Slowly she raised up enough to notice a small-boned yet curvaceous woman with a beautiful face and stylish cap of short red curls standing in the doorway of her hospital room.

One of my best friends? Another unfamiliar face.

"Yes. Of course. Come all the way in."

She wiped her eyes with the bedsheet and sat up while the other woman approached.

"I've been out in the lounge with Cal."

"I—I don't want to see him right now."

"He told me. Don't worry. He didn't send me in here, and he certainly won't do anything you don't want him to do. He loves you too much to alienate you.''

''I wouldn't hurt him purposely, but he means nothing to me. It's hard having him around because I know he's in pain.''

''He said as much, and he's attempting to deal with it. I also realize I don't mean anything to you, either, but there are many people who love and care about you and Cal. You and I were colleagues as well as confidantes. In time you're going to want to talk to someone. You'll have a lot of questions to ask. I want you to know I'll be here for you when that time comes.

''I'm going to leave my business card with you. I've written my cellular phone number on the other side so you can reach me day or night.''

Diana took the card from the other woman's fingers and read:

Annabelle Dunbarton, Private Detective
LFK Associates International
1406 Foothill Parkway
Salt Lake City, Utah

Diana blinked and looked up at Annabelle. ''You say we are colleagues?''

''Yes.''

''You mean, I'm a private detective, too?'' Diana couldn't imagine it, couldn't comprehend it.

''No. You are the glue that holds the whole place together. Roman Lufka is the boss. You're his assistant and right hand. In fact you're the one who screens all the calls that come in. Roman relies on your instincts to help decide which cases to take.''

My instincts?

''There are twelve PI's, but you and I are the only two females on the premises. According to Roman, the agency would fall apart without us. You know the old cliché—ask a woman to get a man's job done?'' Her cat's eyes smiled. ''Anyway, Roman wants you back as soon as possible.

''By the way, he's gorgeous. I mean drop-dead-handsome gorgeous and very married to Brittany, another best friend of both of ours. They have a little boy, Yuri, named after Roman's brother, also another close and dear friend. You and I dote on little Yuri because we both want a baby so badly.''

Diana clutched the sheet in her fist. ''Cal said I've had three miscarriages.''

''Yes, you have. At least you've been able to conceive, and your obstetrician told you that the next time you get pregnant, he's going to sew you up to keep the baby snug inside the full nine months. Cal's a pretty spectacular specimen of gorgeous himself, so you shouldn't have any problems there.''

At the thought of intimacy with the man who claimed to be her husband, Diana shivered, partly from fear, partly from some emotion she couldn't put a name to.

''So far I've been out of luck in the conception department, but of course we haven't been married very long and I'll never give up. When you meet my husband, Rand, you'll see why. He's another version of male gorgeous. Huge. Kind of looks like a lineman for the Green Bay Packers even though he's a computer wizard. It was a case of opposites attracting. When he kisses me, my feet literally don't touch the ground.''

Diana felt herself starting to relax. She turned on her side and rested the uninjured part of her head against the pillow, enjoying Annabelle's loquacious personality.

''Your eyelids are fluttering. That means I've overstayed my welcome. Get some rest, Diana. Call me if you want or need anything.''

''Thank you, Annabelle. For some reason I'm tired all of a sudden.''

''I'm not surprised. It's almost four in the afternoon. Time for you to sleep. What always amazes me is how beautiful you look no matter the hour or the situation. It isn't fair. You're like a golden-haired princess. Do you know, I always wanted hair like yours.

''Cal said he took one look at you and lost his heart. Apparently you felt the same way about him. The kind of love you two share is rare. Even if he's a stranger to you now, don't shut the door on him. It would be the biggest mistake of your life. Cal's one in a million.''

First the nurse, now this woman was singing Cal Rawlins's praises.

After kissing her on the forehead, Annabelle left the room. An odd silence remained following her departure. She emanated such life and vitality, Diana hadn't wanted her to go.

But Annabelle's warning about Cal Rawlins sent

another shiver through her body. She didn't want to think about him just now. She didn't want to remember the agony in those dark brown eyes when she'd told him to go away and leave her alone.

"Mrs. Rawlins? Your husband was worried about you and asked the nurse to send for me."

At the sound of the doctor's voice, Diana opened her eyes. She would have sat up, but Dr. Harkness told her to lie still.

"I'm glad you're here," she began as he sat on the edge of the bed and felt for her pulse. Now she could talk to him about the baby.

He felt her forehead. "Your husband told me you now know the truth about the abandoned infant, how you came to bring it to the hospital for treatment. He's afraid the knowledge has hindered your recovery. You're probably not aware of this, but he's having a difficult time forgiving himself."

"Then he's suffering needlessly because it's not his fault, Doctor. I forced him to tell me. The reason I'm so glad you've come is because I wanted to get your permission to spend time with the baby. I know he's not mine, but since his birth mother hasn't been found, he needs mothering. Let me do it. Please."

She felt his eyes studying her with grave concern. "That baby is under the legal jurisdiction of the court. A set of foster parents will be taking over the infant's care as soon as the pediatrician deems him ready to leave the hospital.

"Even if my hands weren't legally tied, you're in no condition to take care of a baby, not even your own. A little less than twelve hours ago you received a serious head wound which has temporarily robbed you of your memory. You have pain, you're running a temperature. As your doctor, I must insist you stay in bed and get the rest you need.

"I've arranged for Dr. Beal, a staff psychiatrist, to talk to you and your husband first thing in the morning."

Diana's stomach clinched. "I don't want one."

"There are times in everyone's lives when they require professional counseling. I would say this is the most crucial moment of yours and your husband's. You both need help. Dr. Beal can provide the solid guidance to ease you through this traumatic period.

"If he feels it necessary, he'll prescribe medication. Until tomorrow however, I don't advise anything because it might mask some problems which haven't shown up yet. That's why I'm keeping you in the hospital overnight for observation. Tomorrow, depending on a variety of factors, we'll talk about your release."

"What if I don't want to go home with Mr. Rawlins?"

The doctor got up off the bed and grasped her hand. "You see? You need someone to help you work out your fears and formulate a plan. Dr. Beal is that person. Goodnight, Mrs. Rawlins."

Cal had been listening to their conversation through the crack in the door. His fear about her not wanting to go home with him had just been realized. At this point he had a plan of his own.

It wasn't fair. It wasn't moral. It certainly wasn't legal. But he was fighting for his wife.

He hurried back to the lounge and confided his idea to Annabelle who wholeheartedly approved and agreed to help in any way she could.

They waited for the doctor to come and find him. As soon as the doctor had related the substance of his conversation with Diana, Cal ascertained that Diana had permission to walk around the room and use the rest room, if someone was with her. That was all he needed to know before putting the first stage of his plan into action.

While Annabelle waited for Rand to come with their dinner, Cal went back to Diana's room. He could hear her heartwrenching sobs long before he reached the door.

This time he entered without permission. The business about treating her like a sister had gone out the window when he'd told her the truth about the baby. From now on Cal only had one thing going for him, the sheer instinct to survive.

"Diana? The dinner trays are coming up from the kitchen. If you'll promise to eat something first, then I'll take you to the nursery in a wheelchair to see the baby."

At first he didn't think she'd heard him, but slowly her sobbing grew quiet and she lifted her tear-ravaged face to look at him. "Does Dr. Harkness know about this?"

Lord. The hope in her eyes…

"No."

She sat up, alert. "You could get into trouble by going against his express orders."

"If it will make you happy, then I don't particularly give a damn."

She stared at him as if seeing him for the first time. At least for this moment he didn't think he repulsed her quite as much as before. It was a start. *Hell, anything was a start as long as she didn't hate his guts.*

"I promise to eat everything."

"Would you like company for dinner?" He asked the question because he had a feeling she wouldn't be as nervous of him if other people were around.

"Company?"

He nodded. "Annabelle's out in the lounge waiting for Rand. He's bringing dinner for the three of us. We could all eat together, but only if you would like that."

"Oh, yes. She's a very engaging person."

What do you know, Rawlins. Annabelle had gotten through to Diana. It's a step in the right direction.

"You can't help but love our Annie. Now, would you like to freshen up before you greet your visitors?"

"Do I look that bad? No, don't answer that. I can just imagine."

No you can't, darling. You've never realized what a great beauty you really are. Your humility has always been part of your charm. The amnesia hasn't robbed you of that intrinsic quality, thank heaven.

"I only said that to give you something to do. The time must be weighing heavily right now."

"It is." After an overly long pause, "Thank you

for being so thoughtful. Maybe I should at least brush my hair.''

Don't get too overly confident, Rawlins. The situation is so explosive it could blow up in your face at any moment.

He reached in one of the drawers for her cosmetic bag and put it next to her on the bed. "I'll be right back."

Elated by this much progress, he left Diana to her own devices. When he arrived in the lounge he found Rand seated in a wheelchair Annabelle had stolen from one of the empty rooms. He got out of it the minute he saw Cal. In the next instance Rand gave him a fierce hug.

"I know you're in hell. We're here to help any way we can."

Cal eyed the two of them. "You already have. Annie? Diana liked you well enough that we're all going to have dinner together before I wheel her to the nursery."

"Then your idea worked."

He nodded. "For the moment anyway. The baby is the key to my wife's heart. I'll do whatever I have to do to get her to go home with me."

"I just talked to Roman," she informed him. "He's working on an idea he'll discuss with you a little later. Gerard would have been here, but Roman has put him on the case to find the birth mother. If he can't locate her, then she can't be found."

Besides Roman, Gerard was the best PI in the business. Sucking in his breath Cal muttered, "I agree. What would I do without friends like you?"

Annabelle linked her arm through his. "Since you're not alone, it's a moot point. Let's join Diana. Darling?" She turned to her husband. "Oh, good, you've got the food."

Rand grinned and followed closely behind them.

With Annabelle and Rand acting as a buffer, Cal entered Diana's room with a little less trepidation than before. But always in the back of his mind lurked the possibility that she would reject him as she had earlier. For that reason, once they were inside, he let Annabelle take the lead.

To his surprise he discovered his beautiful wife looking through the detective magazine he'd brought with the mail. She had brushed her hair and put on lipstick, several signs that she hadn't yet slipped back into that inconsolable state of tears. Her brave front was something to be grateful for.

"Roman will be glad to know you're studying up on the latest info before you come back to work." Annabelle didn't miss a trick, yet she had a way of prodding Diana that produced a pleasant smile instead of a frown or worse. "Diana? This is my husband, Rand."

Diana put the magazine back on the bedside table, then greeted him politely, but there was no hint of recognition in her eyes.

An orderly brought in Diana's dinner and placed it on the roller table that went across her bed. While Annabelle helped prop her, Cal took that moment to relieve Rand of the sacks and lay things out on one of the tables pushed against the wall. Soon everyone was munching on hamburgers and fries, except for his wife of course.

"Mmm...eggs à la goldenrod. No one told me the hospital had a new chef," Rand quipped. "If I had realized it earlier, I would have phoned in our order for the same thing."

Like clockwork it produced a faint smile from Diana. Cal wondered if the day would ever come when he could evoke that much positive response from his wife. "The doctor says I have to be on a soft diet for the next few days."

Cal happened to know Diana didn't care for eggs prepared in a white sauce over toast, but she was so desperate to be with the baby, she remembered their bargain. Not only did she eat most of her eggs, she finished off the applesauce and drank all her tea without remonstration.

He was thankful the nausea she'd been suffering earlier had abated. Otherwise she wouldn't have been able to force down her meal no matter the incentive. Physically she was much improved since this morning.

Mentally...

How was it that during their careers, boxers could be knocked out dozens of times by vicious blows to the head and fully recover with their memories intact? Yet his wife took one fall on the pavement and in an instant, her past was erased as if it had never been.

Crippling pain immobilized him. He couldn't finish his food.

While Annabelle entertained Diana by pointing out pictures in the wedding album and scrapbook he'd brought to the hospital, Rand took it upon himself to put their papers and cups in the wastebasket. In the process he flashed Cal a look of compassion, then gripped his shoulder as his private way of telling Cal to hang in there.

"Your husband says he's going to take you up to see the baby. Mind if Rand and I walk to the elevator with you on our way out?"

"Of course not."

"Do you want help getting into the wheelchair?"

"No. I can do it myself."

"Then we'll wait for you in the hall."

Thank God for you, Annie. You seem to know instinctively how to handle my wife.

By tacit agreement the three of them left her alone. Diana was so fragile Cal didn't dare linger in case he said or did something to upset her.

Not long after they'd reached the corridor, Cal could see she was trying to open the door. He stepped forward and helped push it back. As she wheeled herself into the hall she thanked him, but there was no eye contact.

At a glance he noticed she'd slipped the silky peach robe he'd brought from the house over her hospital gown. On her feet were her favorite pair of white Italian sandals.

Do your clothes look familiar to you, darling? Would you even tell me if they jogged something in your memory?

"Diana?"

She was forced to look at him. He could tell she hated having to rely on him, but since he was the entree to the baby upstairs, she had little choice but to cooperate.

"Yes?"

"I'm going to push you to the elevator. If anyone stops us or asks questions, let me do the talking, all right?"

"Yes."

"Good. Let's go."

Slowly the four of them moved down the hall and around the corner toward the elevator. Of necessity they had to pass the nursing station. A couple of nurses smiled and said they were glad to learn Diana had eaten her dinner and felt up to a little ride.

She smiled back but he could see her hands clenched together in her lap.

So far, so good.

Rand and Annabelle kept up a lively conversation with her. They ran such beautiful interference, no one would guess Diana regarded them as strangers and *him* as the enemy.

Fortunately there were no people on the elevator when it stopped on their floor. Cal wheeled her inside.

As the doors shut, Annabelle patted Diana's shoulder. "We'll ride upstairs with you, then we have to get home."

The nursery was located on the sixth floor. The quick ride left no time for conversation. When the elevator stopped, several people were waiting to get on. They made way for Cal to push the wheelchair into the hall.

"Don't forget, Diana," Annabelle called out, "you have my number and can phone me at any time."

"I'll remember. Thank you."

Both of them smiled as the doors shut, but Cal caught Rand's private eye signal which said they'd talk later.

"I can hardly wait to see the baby. Where is he?"

For the first time all day she displayed an eagerness and animation reminiscent of the old Diana. Cal didn't think it was possible to be jealous of a tiny infant, but in the last twelve hours he'd discovered a lot of shocking things about himself, none of them worthy of close examination.

"According to the sign, the newborn nursery is down this hall." Without wasting time he pushed her along the corridor till they reached another nursing station. The charge nurse looked up from her charts.

"May I help you?"

"Yes. My wife was the one who fell bringing Baby Doe into the hospital this morning. We understand he's under the lights, but she'd like to see him, even if it's only for a few minutes."

"As long as you're feeling up to it, I don't see why not. Follow me."

Just as Cal said a silent prayer of thanksgiving, Diana darted him a grateful glance. Under the circumstances it was something to cherish.

Continuing on, they passed through a set of swinging doors to a room containing twelve incubators, all of them filled with sick newborns. In some cases one or both parents were in attendance.

"Here he is, yellow as can be, but otherwise healthy. I don't think he likes the lights."

"Oh!" Diana cried out the second she saw him and

got out of the wheelchair before Cal could countenance it. Balancing herself against the side of the incubator, she pressed up against the transparent top. "You precious little darling. Please, can I hold him?"

"I'm sorry. As long as his bilirubin count is high, he has to stay in there, but I tell you what. I'll get you a gown and gloves, and you can put your hands through those holes to give him his bottle. It's time for his next feeding."

"That would be wonderful."

Diana was literally trembling with excitement. Cal feared she would overdo and suffer a relapse of some kind. But her heart was so set on being with this baby, Cal was more afraid of her reaction if she were prevented from seeing him.

"He's so beautiful! How could his mother give him up?"

Cal knew the truth, but he wasn't about to tell her. Not yet anyway. Clearing his throat he said, "She obviously felt she had no choice."

"Why do you think she brought him to my work of all places?"

"She believed the baby would be safe and found quickly." He hadn't told a lie. It just wasn't the whole truth.

Lord—when she found out the birth mother had purposely left that baby for her...

He had moved the wheelchair to the side and stood behind her, ready to catch her in case she grew lightheaded. Afraid his instincts might take over and he'd draw her back against him, increasing her dislike of him, he forced himself to look elsewhere. That's when his gaze fell on the naked infant who moved restlessly under the lights.

He had a thatch of fine dark brown hair and perfect little facial features. His face wore a frown and his mouth was puckered up as if he were ready to cry, but he had to be asleep because he made no sounds. For such a tiny bundle, he had a sturdy body and well-shaped head.

Cal had to admit he was an exceptionally cute little guy. Cuter than he had expected for a child they hadn't made together.

Her last miscarriage had devastated him, but in an effort to comfort her, he'd struggled to keep his own emotions from showing too much. Looking at this baby brought the pain flooding back. Coupled with his grief over Diana's memory loss, he found himself fighting tears.

"If the mother can't be found, I want him. I can't believe he doesn't already belong to me!"

"Diana—"

"I mean it," she broke in. "I love him. I—I hope the police can't trace her. Maybe God will punish me for saying that, but I don't care. You said I found him, so he's *mine*."

His chest heaved from the tumult of emotions growing inside him. Right now there was no reasoning with her. She was running on pure emotion. To her, possession was the proverbial nine-tenths of the law. *Her law.*

Unfortunately the cold hard facts of this case would have to wait until morning because Cal didn't have the courage to face her without the psychiatrist's help.

Diana's terrifying determination to claim this baby for her own was not normal. Cal feared that when she was told that the law might not let her have any say in the child's future, she would need medication to deal with her pain.

Perhaps that was for the best. Maybe then, when her emotions were a little more stabilized, he could convince her that if they lived together as man and wife, they would probably get pregnant again. This time the doctor would perform minor surgery to help her carry it full term.

The only problem with that scenario was the fact that she couldn't stand him to get near her, let alone touch her.

"All right. Here we go." The nurse helped her put on a white gown. "Now the rubber gloves. I'll go around the other side. As soon as I start to feed the baby, you reach in from your side and take over."

A few minutes later Diana's delight in giving the baby his bottle turned to tears of joy as he hungrily sucked on the nipple, draining the three ounces in no time. She crooned to him with all the tender concern of a new mother. Love illuminated her face. Cal had the firm conviction that she'd forgotten he was there. Suddenly the full force of the situation knocked him sideways.

She doesn't know I'm here because I mean absolutely nothing to her. She has no memory of me, therefore she doesn't anticipate a future with me. Nada. *I could literally drop dead and it wouldn't affect her one way or the other.*

Maybe he moaned. Maybe that's what startled her

enough to bring her head around. "If you need to go, that's fine. I'm planning to sit here with the baby tonight."

His hands balled into fists. It was an effort to keep his voice steady. "The nurse won't allow you to stay much longer. I'll wait until she tells you it's time, then I'll make sure you get back to your room safely."

Her proud chin lifted in defiance. "There's no one here to comfort the baby. Surely she'll welcome someone to watch over him."

"That would be true if you were his parent, but—"

"I couldn't feel more his mother if I had given birth to him," she blurted passionately. "Since I brought him to the hospital, I intend to be with him. The poor little thing needs to know his mommy is near."

Cal had to think fast. In going against doctor's orders, he'd created a situation which could grow ugly if he didn't keep a cool head.

"Diana? If you want to spend time with the baby, then you need to prove to Dr. Harkness and the psychiatrist that you're feeling much better and thinking rationally. Let's go back to your room now, before the charge nurse wonders where you are.

"If you insist on staying up here where you shouldn't be, and she tells Dr. Harkness, he'll inform the psychiatrist that your behavior is abnormal. If that happens, I can predict that you'll lose any chance of seeing the baby again."

A long silence ensued.

She looked as if he'd just slapped her in the face.

The last thing he'd wanted to do was be cruel, but Diana was ill. Depending on her reaction to his logic, he would find out just how unstable she'd become since her fall.

To his intense relief she finally placed the empty bottle at the far end of the incubator, then pulled her hands out of the holes. "Good night my darling baby," she whispered in a tear-filled voice. "I'll see you tomorrow. Sleep tight. I love you."

Slowly she removed the gloves and gown. After placing them on a nearby chair, she sat down in the wheelchair. Without saying a word, she allowed Cal to push her out of the nursery.

Except for the nurse who intercepted them and thanked Diana for her help with the baby, the journey back to the fourth floor was made in total silence. Cal knew Diana's masklike countenance camouflaged excruciating pain and disappointment. He could relate.

"Goodness—you two were gone a long time. You must be feeling a lot better, Mrs. Rawlins."

"Yes," Diana murmured to the charge nurse before Cal could speak for her.

"Have you remembered anything yet?"

"No."

That one negative word felt like a red-hot knife slicing him to pieces on the inside. He kept pushing the wheelchair down the hall toward her room.

"You will," the nurse called out. "Just give it time."

Her final comment was meant to be encouraging, but Cal would have preferred it if nothing had been said about her amnesia. He had no idea how Diana felt because she refused to communicate unless it had to do with the baby. For the moment, the little guy upstairs was his wife's only raison d'être.

The situation was volatile. Cal needed to talk to Roman.

When they reached her room, he spoke first to prevent her from telling him to get out.

"I know you don't want any help, so I'll leave. If you should need to get hold of me, the nursing station has my phone number. I'll be here in the morning. Good night."

"Good night. Th-thank you for taking me to see the baby."

"You're welcome. I hope you can sleep. If not, I brought the novel you were reading last night. It's there with the mail that came in yesterday."

Don't linger, Rawlins. Get out of here while the going's good. It took all his strength of will to walk away from her and shut the door. Once outside in the hall, he stood there listening for the inevitable tears. Ten minutes passed.

Nothing.

He didn't know if that was a good or bad sign. His horror of this morning's events had taken its toll on him.

CHAPTER FOUR

"CAL?"

It was Roman. Just the man Cal needed to talk to.

"Has Diana started remembering anything yet?"

"No. Total erasure," he ground out. "I was getting ready to phone you."

"Are you alone?"

"Yes. I'm on my way home from the hospital. The last thing Diana wants is me hanging around."

"Maybe that will change after you hear my news."

His hands gripped the steering wheel tighter. "What news? Heaven knows I could use a glimmer of hope right now."

"Gerard has contacted the birth mother of every living male child delivered at a local hospital within the last six days. No one is missing. Therefore we have to assume the baby's mother delivered elsewhere."

"Do you have any leads on her?"

"No. If you want my opinion, I believe her disappearance is permanent. I've been pondering her note. Her plan to leave the baby with Diana wasn't hatched overnight. She obviously made a thorough study of your wife. She knew her habits and work schedule. It means she gave everything serious thought and is satisfied with her decision."

"She must be young to be so naive! Otherwise she

would have realized Diana has no legal rights to an abandoned baby. The irony of it is, my wife could care less about the law." Cal's voice shook. "She's become obsessed over him. All she wants is to be a mother."

"Maybe she's going to get her wish, temporarily at least."

Cal's heart thudded. "What do you mean?"

"Gerard told his wife the situation. Whitney's planning on being your legal counsel for adoption proceedings. Late this afternoon she met with Judge Cornu in chambers.

"Once he heard about the extenuating circumstances and learned that Chief Bayless had personally vouched for Diana, he granted you two temporary custody of Baby Doe. But there's a condition. A week from today you must show proof that you've begun the process of becoming certified foster parents for the State of Utah. Whitney will have an application for you to fill out when she meets with you tomorrow."

"*Roman—*" Adrenaline spurted through his veins. The miraculous news made it difficult to concentrate on his driving. "You don't know what this means— You can't possibly imag—"

"Yes I can." Roman's deep voice cut him off before Cal could finish expressing his thoughts. "Annabelle and Rand stopped by the house. They said Diana has changed beyond recognition. We're all aware that, for the present, the baby is your only lifeline to her."

"This is going to preserve her sanity, Roman."

Maybe my marriage, God willing. "I don't know how to begin thanking every—"

"Forget it. She's a favorite around here."

How true that was. Diana had a way... No one knew that better than Cal himself.

"You had to have pulled some major strings."

"Why not? I wouldn't own a prime piece of real estate on Foothill Parkway if you hadn't intervened. By anyone's standards it was a miracle. I not only got exactly what I wanted, I made a friend for life. Luckily I'm on good terms with Chief Bayless, and he's crazy about Diana.

"When I explained the situation and showed him the note she found, he said not to worry, that he would take care of the baby's release from the hospital."

"You're incredible."

"Just doing my job. The rest is up to you."

A shudder passed through Cal's body. "That's what terrifies me. Diana doesn't want me in her life."

"The baby is going to buy you the time you need to win her around. She loved you before the accident. She'll love you again."

Annabelle had said the same thing.

"You're as convinced as I am that she's not going to get her memory back."

"I didn't say that."

"You didn't have to. It's a gut feeling on your part. I happen to have the same feeling."

"Don't give up hope, Cal. Memory loss is one of those imponderables. Anything can happen. One day at a time, remember?"

"Thanks to you and the others, I believe I'll be able to get through the next twenty-four hours," he murmured. "When I left the hospital a little while ago, I didn't think that was possible. Let the guys know how grateful I am."

"I will."

"One day you'll know the full extent of my gratitude. Talk to you later, Roman."

"God bless."

"Goodness!" Jane exclaimed as she pushed the wheelchair through the door. "You have so many friends, there aren't enough vases or tables for all these flowers."

They had just come back from X ray. Diana got out of the chair and took a few steps to sit on the edge of the bed. She was amazed to see that during her absence, the hospital room had filled to overflowing with a dozen beautiful arrangements.

Her gaze went to three dozen red roses that dominated the other offerings. Their scent permeated the interior with a sweet perfume. She suspected they were from her husband. The note that accompanied them verified as much.

"One day at a time. Cal."

Though she wished he hadn't bothered, she didn't feel as hostile toward him this morning. If he hadn't broken hospital rules last night, she wouldn't have been allowed to get near the baby, let alone feed him.

She'd spent a restless night debating whether or not to call her husband and plead with him to help her find a way to stay in the hospital a little longer so she could be with the baby. The brief time she'd spent around him proved to her he commanded everyone's respect.

But once she was released from the hospital, would he champion her cause when he found out that she wanted to use her own money to get an apartment?

How soon could she broach him about a divorce?

She didn't have answers to those questions. Not yet. What mattered right now was Tyler. She already had everything worked out down to the colors she would use to convert a second bedroom into a nursery. All that was left to do was convince the psychiatrist that she was fit to care for the baby.

"I'm going to have to get another cart."

"On your way, would you mind finding out my home phone number? I'd like to talk to my husband if he hasn't left the house yet."

"I'd be happy to. While I'm gone, you can read all the cards. Might as well start with this one. Have you ever seen such beautiful blue hydrangeas in your life?"

Diana took the note Jane extended, but her mind was on the baby. The message held little interest for her.

Dearest Diana—
We heard about your accident and are flying out
from New York this weekend. Even if you don't
know us, you need your friends at a time like this.
                                    All our love,
                                    Jeannie and Yuri.

Diana frowned. She wished they wouldn't bother to come, whoever they were.

Frustrated by her inability to remember anything about her past, she placed both notes on the night-stand.

More well-meaning strangers.

Everyone was so kind, thoughtful and sensitive, Diana thought she would go mad. No one understood that Tyler was the only person she needed or wanted.

There was a tap on the door. "Diana?"

That vibrant male voice could belong to only one person. Her pulse quickened when she realized her husband was here sooner than she had expected. Good. He'd saved her a phone call.

"Come in. I'm dressed."

Knowing both doctors would be making rounds before the morning was out, she'd showered early and put on makeup.

This time when he entered the room, she noticed he'd dressed in more casual attire, chinos and a white knit shirt.

"Good morning, Diana. You look like you're feeling better."

"I am. Thank you for the roses. They're lovely."

"You're welcome."

There was an awkward silence. Nervous to broach the subject of the baby for fear he might not be as willing to help her this morning, she asked, "Have you been golfing?"

Her query produced a grimace. "Why do you ask?"

"I don't know. Your clothes maybe."

"I'm not a golfer."

A nervous hand went to her throat. "Was I? A golfer, I mean?"

"No. Neither of us has ever had any interest in the sport."

She got the impression she'd hurt him again without meaning to. It was awful to keep feeling guilty about something she couldn't help. The situation couldn't be allowed to go on much longer. "I—I was just about to phone you."

"Why?"

It was a simple question, but for some reason it unnerved her further.

"To ask you a favor."

After a tension-filled pause, "What is it?"

"If the baby has to stay in the hospital for a few more days, then I don't want to be released yet. I was hoping you could influence the doctor to keep me here so I could help take care of him."

"I've already made arrangements for you to have total access to the baby."

"What?" She stared at him in shock, trying to absorb what he'd just said.

"Actually, I've done more than that. When he's better, how would you like to take him home with you?"

A gasp escaped. "You mean I *can?*"

"That's right."

Her heart raced with sickening speed. "Am I dreaming?"

A little half smile broke the corner of his mouth,

then it disappeared. "No. But before you get too excited, you need to know there are conditions."

"Whatever the conditions, I'll meet them!"

Lines darkened his rugged features. "It's not quite that simple. In this case, we'll *both* have to meet them. That's why I came to the hospital early. I wanted to discuss everything with you before our session with Dr. Beal."

"What do you mean, *both?*" She didn't understand his cryptic response.

"As I told you before, the baby is a ward of the court. When he's well enough to leave the hospital, he'll be placed in foster care. It's the law.

"However, our friend Roman has brought pressure to bear in high places. If you and I agree to become certified foster parents, then the State will allow us to temporarily care for the baby until he is formally adopted."

"But—"

"I know what you're going to say," he interjected quietly. "You don't know me. I'm a stranger to you. The thought of living with me makes you nervous. Unfortunately, it's the only way the court will allow you access to the baby with the possibility of adoption down the road.

"The alternative is separation or divorce. If you want one, I won't fight you. But you need to know that because of your amnesia, the State might never certify you as a single foster parent. If you married again, that would be a different story, but it would be too late for the baby in the nursery upstairs."

Shaken to her foundations, Diana turned away from

him. Not because of the difficulty of the choices presented, but because he was such an incredibly unselfish man.

She might have lost her memory, but she would wager that no one from her past could ever match his generosity of spirit. The extent of his kindness to her was absolutely staggering.

What husband would be willing to stay married to a woman who didn't remember loving him in order for her to mother a baby who meant nothing to him and didn't belong to either of them?

Even more astounding, he had offered her an out. If she didn't want to live with him, he would agree to a separation or divorce rather than force her to stay in a loveless marriage. Instead of exploiting her weakness, he was doing everything he could to empower her.

Had she really been married to such a man for the last four years? How could she not remember him?

"I wish I could offer you a solution that was more palatable." He continued speaking, probably because she hadn't said anything. "Whatever you decide, you need to do it before the psychiatrist comes in.

"Because of your accident, his first impression of your state of mind will go into his initial evaluation. It could be the critical piece of evidence the certification board will study when they consider our candidacy."

"You're right." Again she was stunned because he was trying to prevent her from making any mistakes in front of Dr. Beal. There was no doubt in her mind that Cal Rawlins was a noble human being.

"I've looked into the program." His deep voice reminded her he hadn't finished talking. "The application is only the first step. We would have to attend two evening classes a week for the next month. During each three-hour period, they would teach us the things we have to do to become certified. At the end of the month, a person from social services would come out to the house to interview us and inspect the nursery to make sure everything was adequate.

"Keep in mind that if you wanted to adopt the baby, the court might supersede your wishes and allow him to be adopted by another couple whose name has been on a waiting list for a much longer time. In that event you would have to let the baby go and be prepared to care for another fost—"

"Mr. and Mrs. Rawlins?"

At the intrusion Diana jerked around. A tall, lanky male figure stood in the doorway.

"I'm Dr. Beal. Dr. Harkness asked me to stop by and talk to you."

"We've been expecting you," Cal muttered.

"Good." The psychiatrist stepped inside and shook hands with both of them. "If you don't mind, Mr. Rawlins, I'd like to speak to your wife alone first."

"Of course. I'll go out to the lounge to wait."

Oddly enough Diana would have preferred him to stay in the room. But if she called him back, it might look like she needed him for a crutch.

"You look good for someone who has been through such a traumatic experience. You seem more at peace than I had anticipated. Yesterday Dr.

Harkness painted a little different picture. Has your memory started to return?''

''No.''

He studied her with clinical interest. ''The night charge nurse wrote in her report that there have been no tears, no outward signs of the depression you were in yesterday. You're eating well. Your temperature was normal this morning. How do you account for that?''

Thank heaven Cal had warned her ahead of time.

''M-my husband has been helping me to adjust.''

''I'm glad to hear it. Dr. Harkness will be relieved to know that as well. Yesterday—''

''I know. Yesterday everything frightened me. Not being able to remember the past still frightens me, but people have been kind and understanding, particularly my husband. For some reason today I don't feel quite as threatened by my situation. Maybe that means I've lost my mind completely and don't know it.''

He chuckled. ''Not at all. I would venture to guess that even though you don't know your husband, he has already said and done things to make you feel more comfortable. That's because he knows you better than anyone else. For the time being, it looks as if he's the best medicine you could have.''

''I trust him enough to go home with him.'' *Please don't ask about the baby. I don't want anything to go wrong now.*

''That will alleviate Dr. Harkness's immediate concern for your welfare. It looks like you've taken a major step in the recovery process. Your latest X ray looks good. I see no reason to put you on any medication.

"Under the circumstances I'll tell Dr. Harkness he's free to discharge you at his discretion. However, I would like to see you in my office in a week's time. By then we'll have a lot to talk about. You can arrange your appointment through Dr. Harkness before you go home. If you feel the need to talk to me before then, call me day or night. The nursing station will give you my number."

"Thank you, Dr. Beal. I'll be there."

Until he left the room, she hadn't realized she'd been holding her breath. Once he went out the door, she hugged her arms to her waist, euphoric to think the baby was hers to take home, to love.

For want of something to do while she waited for her husband to return so they could make plans, she read the rest of the cards which had come with the flowers. Reaching for a pen from her handbag, she made notes of who sent what so she could thank everyone later. Cal would supply her with the addresses.

"Yoo-hoo— Diana?"

A feminine voice. Annabelle's? Diana turned toward the door once more. No, not Annabelle. *Another stranger.* A beautiful woman almost as blond as Diana. "Yes?"

"I'm Whitney Roch. Maybe Cal told you about me?"

Whitney Roch.

"You're the attorney! The one who is going to

handle the adoption for us! The one who sent this pretty pink azalea.''

"Yes to everything." She smiled.

"Thank you for the flowers. Please—come in. Does Cal know you're here?''

"He knew I would drop by, but I haven't seen him this morning if that's what you mean.''

"I think he must be talking to one of my doctors. He ought to be in here soon.''

Her concerned blue eyes played over Diana. "You look wonderful, but then, you always do. Still, I realize looks can be deceiving. I can't imagine what it would feel like to be in your shoes, to not remember anything. We've been praying for you.''

Diana felt the other woman's sincerity. "Thank you for that. Were you and I close friends?''

"Yes. Ten months ago I married Gerard, one of Roman's PI's and a good friend of Cal's. The agency is just like one big happy family. We do a lot of things together. As a matter of fact, Gerard and I were going to invite everyone over to our condo this Friday night to watch the basketball playoffs and eat Greek food.''

"Do I like Greek?''

The question sounded so ridiculous they both laughed at the same time. It broke the ice a little more.

"The guys assume we love it. Secretly we hate it because of all the garlic, but we think the sacrifice is worth it because we've got the greatest husbands on earth. Besides, we girls are hard-core basketball fans.''

"We are?''

"You bet. They always kid us that we know more about basketball and could do a better play-by-play sportscast of the games than Wakely and Reeves."

The names meant nothing to Diana.

"You don't remember."

"I'm sorry."

"I'm the one who's sorry for saying anything," Whitney moaned in self-abnegation. "Obviously when you remember something, we'll all know about it. Until then, the last thing you need is more pressure."

Whitney showed a lot of understanding. Diana liked her a lot. Come to think of it, she liked everyone she'd met so far. Before the accident, it appeared her life had been full of kind, wonderful people. That included her husband. Especially her husband.

"I brought the foster parent application for you and Cal to fill out."

Tears stung Diana's eyes. "Thank you so much for helping us get the baby."

"It's my pleasure, particularly when the birth mother meant for you to have him in the first place."

"I don't know about that, but Cal said I found him on the doorstep at work."

"You were supposed to find him."

"*Supposed* to?" she asked, perplexed.

Whitney shifted her weight. "I didn't realize the fall wiped out your memory of the note you found in the box with the baby."

"Cal told me about it."

"So you haven't had a chance to read it."

"*Not yet,*" came the familiar voice of her husband

from the doorway. "Roman turned it over to the police for evidence. They'll eventually return it."

"Cal!"

Diana watched Whitney rush across the room to embrace him in a warm hug which he reciprocated. Only good friends of long standing behaved like that.

"Your wife and I have been getting reacquainted. I'd say she looks pretty terrific."

His enigmatic gaze caught and held Diana's. "I think so, too." For no concrete reason she felt her heart miss a beat.

"Here's the application." Whitney pulled it out of her purse and handed it to him. "When it's ready, call me and I'll come by for it."

"We're indebted to you and Gerard."

"Forget that. Now, I've got to get to the office. Talk to you both later." In a surprise move, she hurried over to kiss Diana's cheek. "That's for the baby." Then she disappeared out the door.

Another silence permeated the room. "She's nice. Everyone has been so good to me."

"We've been blessed with exceptional friends."

Diana nodded.

He folded his arms. "Dr. Beal said you're planning to go home with me."

"I-is that all right with you?"

She heard a sound that could be interpreted several different ways. "The only matter of importance is if it's what you want."

"It is."

His eyes were half veiled. "You must have convinced the doctor. Otherwise he wouldn't have signed the release form.''

''That's because you coached me ahead of time. Thank you for your sacrifice.'' Her voice cracked. ''You'll never know what it means to me.''

His brows formed a bar of dark brown. ''Let's get something straight, Diana. This is no sacrifice for me. You're my wife. I'm in love with you. I want you in all the ways a man can want a woman. I would do anything to keep you in my life.''

After such bald honesty, she felt the shivering start all over again.

''Now that I've cleared up that misconception, I have news about the baby.''

She bit her lip. ''Is he all right?''

''His bilirubin count is going down.''

''Thank heaven.''

''He'll have to stay in the hospital another night. I'm going to pack up your things and take them out to the car. By then maybe Dr. Harkness will have made his rounds.

''Once you're free to leave, we'll go home for a meal and you can check out the nursery to make certain everything is there. Then we'll come back and sit with the baby. How does that sound?''

''I think you can already guess.'' Her voice trembled. She shook her head. ''How will I ever be able to repay you?''

A thunderous expression stole over his features. ''I thought I'd made it clear that gratitude doesn't enter into this. We're married. We have a problem. Like all the other problems that have come along, we'll work it through.''

She watched him as he started to open drawers and gather her clothes. "Have any of them ever been as serious as this?"

"Once I thought you were in love with Roman, that was pretty serious. Especially when I believed he returned your love."

Her eyes rounded. "Isn't he your best friend?"

He paused in the action of opening the closet. "Since when does that stop two people if the attraction is there on both sides?"

The intensity of his question made her realize he had a vulnerable part. Yesterday she couldn't have imagined it.

"Was I unfaithful to you?" she cried in alarm, fearing the answer. He'd gone into the bathroom for her toiletries.

"No, Diana," he said when he came out again. "My own demons were working overtime because after we were married, Roman asked you to come to work for him. I made a good living in the real estate business. There was an assumption on my part that you would want to stay home. Instead you jumped at the opportunity to get out of the house, and I jumped to a faulty conclusion. But we worked it through."

"How?"

"Roman realized I was jealous as hell so he called a meeting of the three of us, said what was on his mind, then forced you and me to do the same. When the truth emerged, I felt like a fool. Interestingly enough, what came out of that conversation strengthened our marriage and our friendship with Roman.''

''What *was* the truth?''

''We fell in love so hard and fast, we married before we knew some of the important things about each other. Like the fact that you wanted a baby right away. I had no idea.

''After a couple of months and you still weren't pregnant, you felt inadequate. Unbeknownst to me you confided your feelings to our good friend Roman who has always been known for his remarkable listening ear.

''He happened to be in the process of building his agency and needed someone to answer the phone. When he could see that you were brooding at home with too much time on your hands, he offered you a job which solved a problem for both of you.''

''Why didn't I tell *you* my fears?''

''Because I had been raised in an atmosphere where the man went to work and the woman was expected to find her fulfillment at home. I had a stubborn side, and you were afraid to hurt me.''

''But I managed to do it anyway.''

''It was nothing more than damaged pride. But the hurt went both ways, Diana. I became moody and difficult. Fortunately we learned from the experience. Since that time we've had a lot of joy.''

''Even with the miscarriages?''

''Even then.''

His image became a blur. ''I'd give anything to remember,'' she whispered in anguish.

"That's wasted energy. We need to concentrate on the baby."

"But do *you* want him?"

"More than you can imagine."

"Even though he's not ours?"

"He will be."

There was no easy way to approach the next question, but because he'd been so honest with her, she felt that she had to ask it.

"Annabelle told me I'm still capable of getting pregnant. Is that true?"

Something flickered in the recesses of his eyes. "You never had trouble conceiving, but you couldn't carry a baby full term. When the obstetrician figured out why, he had a plan to sew you up the next time you got pregnant to prevent another miscarriage. He said it's a routine procedure for women with your problem, and is almost always successful."

When the significance of his words sank in, Diana had to look away. "So there's really nothing to stop us from having our own child."

She heard his sharp intake of breath. "If you're referring to the mechanics alone, then the answer is no. But we're talking about something much more involved here. Without mutual love and desire, then there is everything stopping us from producing a child."

Her heart pounded in her ears. "If you were free to marry someone else, you could have your own baby."

"Probably."

"Yet you're willing to stay married to me and adopt Tyler."

"That's right."

"But it's not fair to *you!*"

After a long pause he said quietly, "I, Calvin Whittaker Rawlins, take thee, Diana Grayson, for my lawfully wedded wife to love and to cherish from this day forward, for richer, for poorer, in sickness and in health, till death do us part."

Her whole body trembled.

"Overnight we've become parents. It's what we always wanted. Now we have a forever kind of job."

But you don't have a wife in the biblical sense of the word. A fresh dart of guilt brought more debilitating pain. She looked everywhere except at him. "What will Roman do?"

"The guys will fill in until he finds someone else. If he grumbles and complains for a while, it's because you were so good at your work. Intuitive. You left some big shoes to fill."

"That's hard to believe. What did I do before we were married?"

"You were a biology major."

"Biology?"

His half-smile was in evidence once more. "I met you soon after you had graduated from the university. You were in the process of selling your grandparents' home so you could relocate to California and accept a job with the Red Cross. That chance meeting changed our liv—"

"Good morning, you two." Dr. Harkness breezed into the room. His entry brought a premature halt to their conversation. "Sorry I'm late. Let me do a quick exam, then I'll arrange for your discharge. If you'd step outside for just a moment, Mr. Rawlins."

Cal headed for the doorway with his arms full. "I'll start loading the car. See you in a few minutes, Diana."

As soon as he was gone, the doctor patted her shoulder. "Dr. Beal was right. You're handling a difficult situation beautifully. Your husband seems much happier, too. How's the head? Still painful?"

"Only if I lie on the pillow in a certain position."

"Good." He did his exam and took her vital signs. "Give it another few days and you won't be able to find the spot. Call me immediately if you start to have flashes of memory, if you have trouble sleeping or are disturbed by bad dreams, if you experience physical symptoms such as nausea or vomiting, dizziness, blurred vision, pain."

"Don't worry. She will," Cal answered for her.

At the sound of her husband's voice, Dr. Harkness looked up. "I'm glad you've come back to hear this, Mr. Rawlins. For the first week I want your wife to take it easy. No housework, no excessive lifting or bending over. Nothing that would cause pressure to her head. Let's give it a chance to heal."

Diana's first thoughts were of the baby. If she couldn't do any of those things for the next seven days, how was she going to take care of him?

Cal must have picked up on her distress. To her amazement he announced, "I'm taking the week off from work. When we get home, my wife's not going to lift a finger."

The doctor looked relieved. "That's excellent. One more piece of advice. Try not to worry too much if your memory doesn't come back right away. Odd as this may sound, your mind has a mind of its own." His comment made her lips curve upward. "It will do what it pleases whenever it pleases. The trick is to be patient."

"I'll try."

"That's all anyone can ask. Good luck to both of you."

Once he'd gone, she turned anxious eyes on her husband. "If he knew we were taking the ba—"

"He doesn't." Cal effectively cut her off. "But even if he did know, he already has my assurance that I'll be home to do whatever needs doing for the baby until you're able to do it yourself."

A whole week under the same roof with him.

At the mere thought, Diana could scarcely breathe.

CHAPTER FIVE

"WHERE are we going?"

The anxiety in his wife's voice startled Cal. When he looked over at her, he noticed one of her hands clutching the edge of the seat. The fingers of her other hand were clawing the armrest.

"Home. What's wrong, Diana?"

"Is it way up there?"

The fear emanating from her caused him to pull his Saab over to the curb. Some of the flowers fell from the back seat of the car to the floor but he ignored them. After shutting off the motor he turned to her. She'd gone pale. He couldn't imagine.

"What is it? What's frightening you?"

"This road. It's so steep. I can't believe we live up there. I don't think I can go on." Her voice quivered.

Cal didn't react right away. He could scarcely credit this was the same woman he'd married. That Diana had been fearless. When none of the other wives would do it, Diana had jumped off the cliffs for the long drop into the deep blue waters of Lake Powell and had come up laughing.

The blow to her head must have affected her vision and balance process in some way. This was one unexpected eventuality he had no idea how to handle.

Oh, darling— If only I could take you in my arms and comfort you.

Perspiration broke out on his forehead. "Do you trust me, Diana?"

Her meek little answer was so long in coming, he almost regretted asking the question.

"Yes."

He exhaled a shuddering breath. "I swear we'll be home in a minute and a half, no longer. If you'll undo your seat belt and slide closer, you can burrow into me. That way you'll have something to hold on to, and you won't have to look."

Ominous silence invaded the car's interior while Cal waited for her response. An eternity seemed to pass before he heard a click and felt her bury her face against his shoulder.

His heart melted when he realized the courage it took to do as he suggested despite her fear.

"Just cling to me," he urged, and they were off once more. By the time he drove the car into the garage a minute and twenty seconds later, her fingernails had dug right through the knit fabric to score the flesh of his upper arm.

"We've arrived. You can open your eyes now."

With reluctance she lifted her head and sat back in the seat. The panic was still there in her eyes. "H-how high up are we?"

He had to think fast.

Their sprawling, desert-style house sat on three choice acres of scrub oak property a thousand feet above the valley floor. They had hired an architect to design a plan that fit the landscape and took full advantage of the breathtaking view.

Arlington Heights was located on the northeast end of the city. Every window gave out on a sweeping panorama of earth and sky. But the shutters in the master bedroom were still closed. If he carried her there from the front door, she wouldn't have a chance to see the view.

"It doesn't matter."

Without hesitation he levered himself from the car and came around her side. Not giving her a chance to argue with him, he lifted her bodily from the car. "Put your arms around my neck. You'll be safe in your bed before you know it."

Instead of going through the inner door to the kitchen, he headed back out of the garage and strode along the walkway to the front door. Her terror was so great, it was like carrying a full-size wooden figure.

"We're almost there."

He nearly ran with her as he passed through the front foyer, around the corner and down the hall leading to the semidark master suite. Without pausing to turn on lights, he took a few swift strides across the plush carpet to their queen-size bed.

After settling her back against the pillows, he turned on the reading lamp. She had buried her face in her hands, as if she were afraid to look at him. He could barely make out her words of apology between her sobs. "Y-you must think I'm o-out of my mind."

Without conscious thought Cal sat on the edge of

the bed and gathered her into his arms, rocking her back and forth, kissing the top of her silken head. "You're in hell. Who wouldn't be? How can I help you?" The moisture from her tears was seeping into the front of his shirt.

"I don't think I can s-stay here."

He held her tighter. "Because we're up high?"

"Yes. Even though I can't see out, I feel like we're going to f-fall down."

"Then we'll go."

Still holding her with one arm, he reached for the phone with his free hand and called Brittany, Roman's wife. Thankfully she answered on the third ring. Without preamble he asked if he and Diana could come over right away.

Brittany didn't ask any questions. She sensed something was wrong and simply told him she would be expecting them whenever they could get there.

He murmured his thanks, hung up the receiver, then carried Diana out of the room and the house. His wife was experiencing some form of vertigo. If it didn't disappear by the time they reached Roman's home, which was nestled in a wooded area at the foot of Mt. Olympus Cove, then he would take her back to the hospital.

As soon as he had the opportunity, he would phone Dr. Harkness to find out if this was a normal side effect of a head injury, but he didn't want to discuss it in Diana's hearing.

When they were ensconced in the car once more, she didn't need any prompting to hold on to his arm and hide her head. If it weren't such a nightmarish situation, he would have been gratified that she felt comfortable enough to turn to him and cling.

As soon as they reached the valley floor he said, "You can open your eyes now. We're headed for Roman's house. There are no hills, so you don't have to worry about heights."

Slowly she released her stranglehold on his arm and lifted her head. To his relief she took a deep breath and sat back in her seat. The panic on her face had vanished as if it had never been. *Thank God.*

"Feeling better?" he asked unnecessarily.

She nodded. "Much."

"That's good."

Her hands twisted together.

"Thank you for being so understanding."

Diana, Diana...

"You're welcome." He decelerated as they approached a light. "There's a drive-thru ahead. I could do with something to drink. How about you? Are you thirsty?"

"Do you think they have lemonade?"

He had to brace himself not to react. Diana was a Coke addict. Like everyone else at the agency who subsisted on caffeine, she thought lemonade was insipid and would rather go without than drink it.

The fall had changed her in incomprehensible ways. He never knew what to expect from one minute to the next. Every new aspect of her came as a shock.

"I'm sure they do." It was on the tip of his tongue to tell her they served her favorite fajita rollups. At the last second he thought the better of it. In her fragile state she didn't need any added pressure.

When he placed their order, he asked her if she wanted something to eat. She said she wasn't hungry. He wasn't, either. He'd lost his appetite when the vertigo attacked her.

After handing her the lemonade, he took a long swallow of his Coke and they drove off.

"Cal?"

What was coming next? He groaned inwardly. "Yes?"

"How can we take the baby home if I can't live there?"

He had already anticipated that problem. "It's very simple. We'll move into another house."

"But—"

"There are no buts. Real estate is my business. My company has hundreds of vacant houses listed right now. We can pick the one we want today, call the movers to pack our things, and move in tomorrow."

In fact, if he remembered correctly, a property across the street from Roman's had just been listed with his company. He hadn't seen it yet, but it might be the perfect solution. With one phone call, his attorney could buy it for him today. Diana would have friends within walking distance.

"That's asking too much. I can't let you do that."

His jaw clenched. "A house is a house, Diana. A family is something else again. Do you honestly think I give a damn where we live?"

"But I feel so guilty because you're having to make all the sacrifices."

Careful, Rawlins, before you blow it.

"When we lost the baby a few months ago, I suffered more than you know. It's like a miracle that this little guy has come into our lives. I'll do anything to keep him. If it means a move, then so be it."

Her head was bowed. "I don't know what to say. Thank you hardly seems adequate."

"Why do you insist on thanking me for something we both want?"

After a brief silence, "I'm sorry."

"Sorry enough to stop?" he asked in a teasing voice.

"I'll try."

She started sucking on her straw. *Another aberration.* The old Diana had no use for them. She always took off the lid and drank right out of the cup. Watching her now, he realized that if her spirit weren't encased in her familiar outer shell, he wouldn't know her.

Thirty-six hours had passed since her fall. In that period of time she'd had no flashes of memory. He didn't know why, but more and more he was coming to believe that the Diana he'd married would never return. A new person inhabited her body. Getting to know her was going to be a long, complicated process. But there was no question that he loved her body and soul.

The only wrinkle was Diana herself. She might never fall in love with him. *What then, Rawlins?*

He couldn't handle that possibility. In fact he refused to entertain it.

"We've arrived," he muttered as they pulled into Roman's driveway.

She looked all around. "It's very secluded, isn't it?"

"Roman guards his privacy jealously. Does it make you apprehensive?"

"No."

"Something's bothering you."

"Is Roman going to be here?"

"Probably not until later. Why?"

"I don't know. I guess I'm feeling a little nervous to meet the person I used to work for."

Cal couldn't help but be intrigued. "For what reason?"

"Because I feel so foolish not remembering anything."

"You don't feel foolish with me, do you?"

"Not anymore."

Thank heaven for that.

"Roman's the best. He's the easiest person in the world to be around. There's nothing to worry about. As for Brittany, she's a sweetheart."

Before he'd helped Diana to the front door, Roman's ash-blond wife came running toward them followed by their cat, Clouseau. Unlike everyone else, Brittany had no reservations as she introduced herself, then hugged Diana and invited her inside the house like nothing untoward had happened.

"Yuri just woke up from his nap. I realize you

don't remember him, but he's going to be thrilled to see you. He calls you Di-Di.''

"Is Yuri a Bulgarian name?'' Cal heard her ask Brittany as they went down the hall to the nursery.

"Russian.''

"You're married to a Russian?''

"Well, he's part Italian, too.'' She grinned. "But I'm afraid the Russian takes over when his brother Yuri comes to town.''

"He's the one who sent us the blue hydrangeas,'' Diana reminded Cal.

Cal could be thankful that there was nothing wrong with her memory since the accident.

When they entered Yuri's room the seventeen-month-old was standing in his crib making noises.

"Hi, little sweetie. Look who's here? It's your auntie Di and your uncle Cal.''

"Di-Di,'' he said several times and did patty-cake with his hands.

Cal leveled his gaze on his wife. She loved Yuri. Maybe seeing him would trigger something in her mind.

"Where did he get such black, curly hair?'' Though she remarked on him, she didn't reach for him as she would have done in the past.

Brittany must have noticed the change in Diana but she didn't let it show as she picked him up and started to change his diaper on the twin bed near the crib. "He's a dead ringer for Roman, aren't you? The apple of his eye.'' She blew on his tummy until he shrieked with laughter.

To Cal's surprise Diana turned to him rather than

the baby. "Tyler has a little hair, doesn't he, but it's brown."

"Kind of like his new daddy's," Brittany interjected, then winked up at Cal. "I'm so happy for you two. Roman's told me everything. I understand you'll be taking him home from the hospital tomorrow." By now Yuri was dressed and ready to play.

"We hope so," Diana murmured in a wistful tone. "Today his bilirubin count was down."

"I'm sure another night under the lights will do the trick."

"That ought to give us enough time to find a house."

Brittany stared dumbfounded at Cal.

"Since the fall Diana can't handle heights," he explained. "We've decided to look for a place *without* a view."

When the information computed, Brittany blurted, "The house across the street hasn't sold yet!"

"I was thinking of that one. Have you been in it?"

"Several times. It's all on one floor and spacious. The owner used the room off the master bedroom for a study. You could easily convert it to a nursery."

"Diana? Would you like to go over and see it?"

"Yes. Very much."

Her face looked more animated than before. He could tell the idea appealed.

Bless you, Brittany. Your friendly, natural manner has already won my wife's trust.

Elated by this much progress, he reached for Yuri.

"Come on. Give your uncle Cal a hug." The little boy patted his cheeks. Together the four of them headed toward the front door.

"They were such good neighbors," Brittany chatted as she walked out of the house arm in arm with Diana. "But now that they've moved, Roman and I have been hoping a family with young children would move in. Wouldn't it be perfect if you lived across the street from us?"

Her exuberance warmed Cal's heart.

"Maybe Cal hasn't had a chance to tell you that I'm expecting again."

"I think Annabelle mentioned it. When are you due?"

"December. It's still a long way off. Just think— we could take the children for long walks in their strollers. The elementary school is only a few blocks away, and there are two parks close by. All the land here is heavily wooded. It's beautiful, and in summer it stays cooler even when it's hot everywhere else."

"You should be teaching my sales staff how to sell. When you're ready to come to work for me, just say the word and you're hired!" Cal teased.

Brittany chuckled. "That would be outrageous. Me working for you, and Diana for Roman. Fortunately, we women have our babies to look after, so you poor men are going to have to continue hunting for buffalo by yourselves."

Diana actually laughed out loud.

The familiar sound haunted Cal because it was the one and only reminder of the adoring woman who'd made love to him yesterday morning as dawn crept into their bedroom.

Would there ever be another morning like that again? Would she ever cry out her love to him over and over again?

"Cal?"

His head jerked around.

Brittany eyed him with concern. "If you don't have the key to the real estate box, I can run back to the house for one of Roman's devices to help you get in through the back door. After all, it's your company that is showing the house."

"I've got the key. Thanks anyway." Still holding Yuri, he reached in his pocket with his free hand for his key ring.

"I was just telling Diana that whatever house you decide on, she can stay in our guest room with Tyler until the house is ready to be moved into. I've got everything she'll need for the baby until then."

The sleeping accommodations.

You've just solved the major problem for my wife. I should be on my knees to you, Brittany.

"You're a generous soul." He turned to Diana. "Is that all right with you, or would you prefer to stay in a hotel?" He stared into eyes that looked a velvety green beneath the canopy of leaves.

Red stained her cheeks.

Cal couldn't remember the last time he saw his wife blush. Maybe on their wedding night. Her vulnerability was a revelation.

"I'd enjoy staying with Brittany." Suddenly she

acted nervous and avoided his gaze. "Yuri?" she said too brightly. "Do you want to come to me?"

Cal held him back. "Remember Dr. Harkness's warning? In a week, you can do whatever you like."

"I forgot."

As he opened the front door, he relived that same sinking sensation he'd experienced yesterday after the call from the hospital. There were still so many obstacles to face. Even then he had no promise that she would ever come to love him.

He groaned under the weight of his grief. This was only the second day...

CHAPTER SIX

"DIANA? Brittany told me to tell you that Tyler's still sleeping, so not to rush back. Where do you want the baby dresser to go?"

"Roman—" she cried in exasperation. "You're not supposed to be here. You and Brittany have had to put up with too much as it is. We've invaded your home for a whole week, kept everyone up nights with the baby. We'll never be able to return your generosity."

"That makes us even because I'll always be in your debt for helping me get my agency off the ground when I first moved here from New York. Now tell me what to do with *this*. The van has arrived. Cal's busy out front directing the movers."

There was no stopping Roman. As she had come to find out over the last seven days, the handsome ex-Green Beret, ex-police lieutenant et cetera, et cetera was as dynamic a force as her own husband. It was no wonder they were best friends.

"The nursery is the second door down the hall on your right. It adjoins the master bedroom."

"I'll find it."

"Diana?"

She whirled around, no longer bothered by any attendant dizziness. Yesterday Dr. Harkness had declared her physically fit to resume her normal duties.

He said that in time she would probably overcome her vertigo. She remembered hearing the doctor commend Cal for making the decision to move into another house since Diana had enough on her plate dealing with the memory loss without trying to overcome her fear of heights at the same time.

"Rand!" He was holding the crib that Cal had set up temporarily at Roman's. "You're here, too?"

"It's moving day. We wouldn't be anywhere else. Point me in the right direction will you, sweetheart?"

She gave him the same instructions as Roman. As she watched his retreating back, her throat swelled with emotions she'd had trouble holding back. Their friends had to be the choicest people on earth.

Everyone had dropped by Roman and Brittany's house bearing food and flowers, gifts for Tyler. The outpouring still continued. Between all the excitement, not to mention the constant care of their new baby, she hadn't had time to dwell on her memory loss.

She didn't want to. It frightened her.

Thankfully no one ever talked about the accident. Cal, particularly, was careful to leave the subject alone. Sometimes she felt his eyes on her while she was feeding the baby. She sensed he was waiting for a sign that she had recalled something. *She never did.*

At night when she said her prayers, she begged God to restore her memory. So far, the past was a blank page. Though her husband would deny it, her inability to remember their marriage had to be hurting him terribly. On occasion she felt his pain, even glimpsed it when something came up she should have remembered, and didn't.

Except for pictures from the scrapbooks, she had no way of knowing what she was like before the accident. Brittany said there were dozens of videos she could watch, but Diana didn't have the courage to look at them yet.

It was bad enough imagining that the person she'd become was a great disappointment to her husband. Day after tomorrow would be her first appointment with Dr. Beal.

He'd been prophetic when he'd said they would have a lot to talk about. As each day passed, she was feeling more and more inadequate. Sometimes she thought she had to be the world's worst mother. Cal would see her frustration and quietly take over until she calmed down. He never complained.

Because of her phobia, they couldn't live in the house he'd had built for them. He said it didn't matter, but she knew that couldn't be true. Who wouldn't be upset if their whole world had been turned upside down overni—

"Ma'am? Where do you want the piano to go?"

She'd been so deep in thought, she hadn't realized the movers had come into the living room. When she caught sight of the ebony harp lying sideways on the dolly, she realized they'd brought in a baby grand.

Was Cal a pianist?

"O-over in that far corner, I guess. Away from the windows," she said absently, intrigued by the possibility that he had a talent he'd never mentioned. He rarely talked about himself.

Do you ever try to draw him out?

She already knew the answer to that. Her guilt was growing in quantum leaps.

"Diana? I've finished the wiring in the hall. Come and see how the master panel works."

Annabelle had taken it upon herself to install all the latest gadgets to keep their house protected from burglars, or worse. Until Roman showed Diana the list of surveillance cameras and listening devices manufactured by Yuri Lufka's company, she had no idea what was available to the public in the way of protection.

"Now your house is invader-proofed!" her red-headed friend said with a saucy grin. "It's pure state-of-the-art. Just flick this switch and not even Cal will be able to get in if he comes home from the office later than you think he should."

Diana burst out laughing. "Do you have all this done to your house, too?"

"More," Rand chimed in, giving his wife a loving squeeze around the waist that lifted her feet a few inches from the carpet. "I made sure she burglar-proofed our place before we got married. Since then, she has added a few items. It's a miracle I haven't suffered from cardiac arrest yet, *Lois.*"

"True, *Ray.*"

A special look passed from one to the other. They chuckled before he lowered his head and kissed her. Obviously it was a private joke between husband and wife. Two people who blatantly adored each other.

A stabbing pain pierced Diana's heart. There was none of that between her and Cal. In order to enjoy

treasured private moments, you both had to remember the same things.

Unable to watch their happiness any longer, she turned to leave, then halted. Cal stood a few feet away gazing at her. He held a packing box so she couldn't see all of his face. But the bleak look in his eyes led her to believe he'd been there long enough to witness the by-play between Rand and Annabelle.

Diana wished he hadn't been anywhere around just now. She was cognizant of the fact that no matter where he looked, there were poignant reminders of the love they'd once shared. She couldn't stand to see him hurt.

He was so good. He was trying so hard.

"I-if you'll excuse me, I'm going to run across the street and check on Tyler."

"I just did," Cal muttered. "He's still asleep. Actually, I'd like your input on something. In the other house, you and I shared an office. Do you want the same arrangement here, or would you like your computer set up in the master bedroom? It's roomy enough in there to hold your equipment."

"I don't understand. The master bedroom is *your* room."

He shook his head. "It makes more sense if you sleep there since it's closer to the baby."

"That's ridiculous," she blurted, feeling her cheeks grow hot. "The other bedroom is only a few more steps down the hall. I wouldn't know how to use a computer and I don't need a big room. Stop being so kind to me. It's killing me!"

Before the words left her lips she wished to God

she'd never said them. A mask had stolen over his face, robbing it of expression.

"I'm sorry—" she cried out, horrified by what she'd done. "I didn't mean that the way it sounded. You *know* I didn't."

He stayed frozen in place. His stillness told her she'd hurt him irrevocably.

"Please understand— I can't bear it that my accident has turned your life inside out. Don't you realize it would help me more if I thought you weren't giving up so much? Try to put yourself in my place. If our circumstances were reversed, I have a feeling you wouldn't allow me to sacrifice *anything*." She hated the quiver in her voice.

A dark shadow passed over his features. "You're right. I wouldn't," he said in a voice she didn't recognize. "You've made your point."

"Cal—" she called after him, wanting to ease the tension between them. Unfortunately the movers chose that moment to come down the hall, robbing her of the opportunity to ameliorate an ugly situation.

One you created, Diana.

If it weren't for your husband, you wouldn't have your baby.

You wouldn't have a home to come home to. You wouldn't have any friends.

You owe him everything.

How could you treat him like this?

What kind of a person are you?

"In case you hadn't noticed, it's late, bud. The crickets are chirping. You've done the work of ten men today. Why are you still out here?''

"You mean instead of being in bed with my wife who has about as much interest in me as she does that shade tree?'' Cal jerked the last cushion out of the packing box and fastened it to the patio chair. "Sorry, Roman. Right now I'm—''

"Tell me about it.'' Roman cut him off. "I've been there, remember?''

"This isn't going to work. I can't do it right with Diana.''

"Then stop trying. Just be yourself.''

He got up from his haunches. "She said the same thing in so many words.''

"You've made progress. She's home with you.''

"*That's* a miracle,'' he ground out.

"Nobody pointed a gun at her head. She came of her own free will.''

"You're forgetting Tyler.''

"Of course he's a big part of it. But I've been watching her over the last week. She's very assertive in her likes and dislikes. If she didn't want to be here, she wouldn't be. Remember the first morning you brought the baby home from the hospital?''

"How could I forget? Once the nurse placed Tyler in Diana's arms, I wasn't needed.''

"Brit behaved exactly the same way with Yuri when I brought them home. I felt left out, too. But that stage lasted about four hours before she remembered I was around. Diana was no different.

"What I haven't told you is that later in the day, when you slipped away to your old house to get things ready for the packers, she suddenly noticed you were missing and asked us where you were. You could tell she was hurt that you hadn't told her you were leaving."

"Look, Roman— I appreciate what you're tryi—"

"I'm not finished. There's something else you should know."

An odd nuance in Roman's tone caught Cal's attention. "What is it?"

"Remember that same night when you got a phone call from me telling you to come back to our house and sleep on the Hide-A-Bed?"

"Yes. You said Diana needed help with the baby."

"I lied."

"What?"

"Around eleven, just before I phoned you, Diana knocked on our bedroom door and asked when you were coming back."

"You mean she actually remembered I was alive?" His voice grated.

Roman squeezed his shoulder for a minute before letting it go. "We told her you were planning to sleep at the old house until the new one was ready. You could have heard a pin drop. She went pale at the news.

"I asked her if she was ill or needed help with the baby. She said no, begged us to forgive her for the disturbance, then she shut the door and went away.

"Brit and I took one look at each other and realized that Diana didn't feel secure without you in the house. Her anxiety was tangible, Cal. That's when I phoned you. She became a different person the second you arrived. Happy.''

''I must have been the last person to know it.''

''That's because you're too upset to read the signs. For instance, you probably weren't aware that your wife asked Brit to keep Clouseau away from the nursery. Even though we had assured her that Yuri had always been safe with the cat around, she wasn't convinced.''

''I didn't know that.''

''Why should you? It wasn't important. A lot of people don't like pets near newborns. My point is, your wife wasn't afraid to speak up. She may have lost her memory, but she knows what she wants and doesn't want.

''Have you considered her outburst today could be a sign that she'd like to get on a closer footing with you? If you keep trying to defer to *her* wants, how can she ever find out what *you* want?''

He sucked in his breath. ''I made my wants perfectly clear before we left the hospital.''

''And?''

''She broke down and said something about wishing she could remember.''

''But you didn't scare her off, otherwise she wouldn't be sleeping under the same roof with you tonight. Maybe she needs more convincing. Brit says that if she were in Diana's shoes, she'd probably be afraid you wouldn't like the new version of her as well as the old.''

''That's insane!''

''I agree. However I've learned never to underestimate my wife's intuition. She's inevitably right when it comes to figuring out the female psyche. Promise me you'll think about what I've said.

"Oh—before I forget. The police sent the birth mother's letter back. It's yours." He pulled a folded paper from his pocket and handed it to Cal. "In case I haven't said it yet, I couldn't be happier that you're living across the street from us. If you want the truth, Brit and I are ecstatic."

"Ditto," Cal whispered emotionally, clapping his friend on the shoulder before Roman said good-night and walked off.

Diana had been counting the minutes until Cal came back in the house. Though she couldn't hear their conversation, she knew Roman had been out on the patio with him. The two men shared a close bond.

As grateful as she was to Roman and his wife, she couldn't help but wonder what they really thought of her. Right now they were doing what any close friends would do, rallying around Cal until the crisis had passed.

But what if the crisis never ended? What if she never regained her memory? How long would it take before she alienated everyone because she wasn't the same person she used to be? How long before Cal decided he wanted a divorce?

Tortured by questions she couldn't answer, she slipped the peach robe over her nightgown and padded into the nursery to check on her sweet little angel. He was filling out more and more every day. She couldn't wait to find out what color his eyes were going to be. At the moment they were sort of muddy. Secretly she hoped they would turn brown like Cal's, dark and velvety with long black lashes. When he smiled, her husband had the most beautiful eyes she'd ever seen.

Funny how Annabelle had described Roman as drop-dead gorgeous. Though Diana agreed that their boss was fascinating in a European kind of way, and certainly Rand was attractive, she much preferred Cal's rugged looks and physique, the ultimate Western male.

The ultimate human being. Tyler couldn't have a better role model for a father.

And a better husband for you?

It had only been a week, but she had begun to realize that Annabelle had spoken the truth about Cal. He was a man in a million. He'd already proven his worth in so many ways, Diana was humbled by it.

The real issue here was the matter of her *own* worth. How was she measuring up in her husband's eyes?

Not very well. Not very well at all. The incident in the hall this afternoon was a case in point. She'd been suffering ever since, waiting for the time when she could talk to Cal and apologize for her insensitivity. But depending on how late Roman stayed, she might have to wait until morning.

This was one time when she wished Tyler were awake. His warm little body always gave her great comfort. But he was sleeping too peacefully for her to think of disturbing him. With reluctance, she tiptoed out of the nursery and darted toward her room.

"Oh!" she cried as she ran into something large and masculine in the darkness. Cal must have just come in from the back patio. His hands went to her upper arms to steady her in a firm grip.

"Forgive me, Diana. You hurried out of the room so fast you surprised me. Are you all right?"

"I'm f-fine," came the breathless lie. Though he'd been working hard all day, she could still detect the pleasant scent of the soap he used. "Are you okay?" she asked to cover the chaotic state of her emotions.

During those few seconds when her body had collided with his, she'd felt the pounding of his heart. The male hardness of his broad chest and thighs came as a revelation. She prayed he hadn't felt her tremble before he let her go.

"I couldn't be better. How's our son?"

"He's perfect. He eats everything, burps exactly the way he should, and sleeps. I've always heard horror stories about hard it is dealing with a newborn baby, but Tyler never fusses or anything. Do you think that's normal?"

"I think we're lucky. Since we're on the topic of the baby, come in the kitchen with me. Roman brought something by I want you to see." There was an air of excitement about him.

Intrigued, Diana followed him down the hall and around the corner to the other part of the house. He flicked on the light of the spacious kitchen.

She'd tried to get everything in order, but two boxes labeled Glasses And Bowls still sat on the cream-colored floor tiles waiting to be unpacked. She would open them in the morning.

He placed a folded piece of paper on the round glass top of their dinette set.

"What is it?" she asked as he reached in the fridge for a cola.

"Read it and find out."

It looked like a letter of some kind written on lined paper. Suddenly she connected it with Roman's nocturnal visit and realized it was the note left with the baby.

"Dear Diana," it began.

She gasped softly, then lifted her head. Her gaze collided with Cal's.

He eyed her searchingly. "What is it? Do you remember reading it before?"

The hope in his eyes, the intensity of his question made her feel guiltier than ever.

"No. I'm sorry."

"Don't apologize. When you cried out like that, I thou—"

"You thought the note had triggered a memory." *He hoped this would produce a miracle. He wants me to be the way I used to be. He doesn't like me the way I am.* "I wish it had," she whispered in pain. "The reason I gasped is because this note was written to *me personally.*"

"That's right," came his gravelly response.

"Now I understand what Whitney meant when—"

"Just read it," he admonished gently. "Then you'll know everything."

He's trying so hard to pretend he's not upset.

Her hands shook as she started to digest the contents. By the time she'd come to the last line, she was sobbing. The whole page had turned into a blur.

"Are you angry with me?"

Surprised by his question, she lifted her tear-stained face to him. "Why would you ask that?"

"Because I didn't tell you the whole truth about the letter in the beginning."

She smoothed an errant lock of hair out of her eyes. "Of course not. Besides, I understand why you didn't. On the day of my accident I had already claimed the baby to be mine by divine right. If I'd had this note in my possession, I would have been a worse basket case than I am right now."

"Don't talk that way about yourself, Diana. You've survived an ordeal few people have ever had to endure. Everyone is in awe of your courage. I—" He paused. "I admire you more than you know."

She'd heard the slight hesitation. No doubt he'd had to search to come up with something complimentary in order not to hurt her feelings.

"You're very kind, but I've needed something to bring me down to earth in a hurry. This note has done it."

His face darkened with lines. "What do you mean? I was hoping you would be thrilled that the birth mother picked you out of everyone else to take care of her child."

"You mean *us*. She mentioned you in her letter, as well. But it's a two-edged sword, isn't it? Whoever Tyler's mother is, she knows who we are and where we are. She can come back for him anytime she wants. More and more I'm understanding the speech you made at the hospital about being prepared if we had to give him back later.''

He took a step toward her, his expression implacable. "Everything has a bottom line. I said those things to get them out of the way, but I don't believe they'll happen. Neither does Roman, and I trust his gut instincts over anyone else's.''

Diana was fast losing another battle with tears. "What if things don't work out and someone else adopts him first?''

"That's why we have Whitney on the job. She's not going to let us down if she can possibly help it. But we have to do our part. Our first priority is to get certified as foster parents. The class starts tomorrow night.''

"But maybe her efforts won't be good enough. We could still end up with *nothing!*''

Her cry reverberated throughout the kitchen. When the sound died down, a disquieting silence took its place. Cal's eyes narrowed. "If that's the way you really feel, then we should call social services in the morning to come and get Tyler.''

"No!" She brushed at her tears with the palms of her hands. "You don't want that and neither do I. I-it's just that I'm so frightened.''

"I know. This is a time when we need to exercise our faith. Perhaps we should do as the birth mother suggested.''

Diana frowned, not comprehending.

"She asked us to take Tyler to church. By fulfilling her wish, maybe we'll find the comfort we need.''

Church. "Did we—did you and I attend one?''

He nodded. "The same one where we were married. But we couldn't go on a regular basis. The real estate business doesn't stop for Sundays. Neither does the Lufka agency. Sometimes Roman needed you to cover the phone."

"I think I'd like to go, except that I'd prefer someplace different."

He set the can on the sink. "Why? Have you remembered something?"

There was that question again. It haunted her every time he asked it.

"No. I wish that were the reason, but it isn't. I just can't handle the idea of meeting a lot of people who knew me before my accident."

After a brief pause, "I don't relish the idea of facing a barrage of questions myself. So we'll find a church out here in the Cove where no one knows us. We'll start fresh."

"You mean it? Are you sure it's all right?"

"Diana—" The exasperation in his voice meant she'd said the wrong thing again. "Worship was an important part of our lives. It meant a lot to Tyler's birth mother, as well, or she wouldn't have mentioned it in her note. Do you honestly think I care which church it is?"

His sincerity won her over. "No. Of course not. I'd like to find one and go this Sunday if we can."

"So would I." Like the sun peeking out from a dark cloud, she saw his eyes gleam with a light that hadn't been there before. Her response had pleased him.

Diana couldn't remember attending church, but she

felt deep inside it was the right thing to do for them, for their son.

"Diana? There's one more thing."

Her heart turned over. "What is it?"

"Will you let me get up in the night to feed Tyler? I'd like some time with him."

His request should have come as a relief. Instead her reaction was a mixture of surprise and disappointment because she'd thought he was going to ask her something that didn't have anything to do with the baby.

"Of course," she answered too brightly. "The only reason I didn't suggest it before was because you've been working hard to get us moved in. I wanted you to have your sleep while we were staying at Brittany's."

"I know, and I appreciate it. But I need to get better acquainted with my son."

"He needs you, too. Good night, Cal. Thank you for showing me this letter," she added quietly. "I— I want you to know that I *am* thrilled she picked us."

Feeling a prickly heat sensation, she hurried out of the kitchen, afraid to admit to herself that she enjoyed being around her husband, that she craved his company more and more.

A week ago she'd pushed Cal away when he'd tried to kiss her. She'd contemplated asking him for a divorce.

How in seven days could everything have changed so completely? What was wrong with her that she could be jealous of the baby who deserved his daddy's complete attention for one night?

* * *

"Come on, Tyler. Give your old dad a burp. That's it."

While he patted the warm tiny back, Cal walked around the nursery rubbing his chin against the baby's head. He could smell Diana's perfume mixed with the baby powder. The scent intoxicated him.

"We've made progress today, son. It's beginning to feel like we're a family. Last week I wouldn't have given us a chance in hell. You probably don't know what that means, so I'll explain.

"Last week, your mommy couldn't stand me to be in the same room with her. She told the doctor she didn't want to go home with me when he released her from the hospital. Yet seven days later here we are in our new house, all three of us.

"It's a good omen, Tyler. Let's just pray this new state of affairs isn't temporary," he said as he kissed the baby's neck where Diana's lips had been.

Carefully he put the sleeping infant back in the crib and covered him with a light blanket. *God knows I couldn't handle it if anything went wrong now.*

CHAPTER SEVEN

"THIS will be our last class before someone from the certification board comes to your home next week and makes the final inspection. Therefore we'll use the remaining minutes to go over the list again.

"Every home must be child-proofed. All harmful chemicals in kitchens, bathrooms, garages, storage rooms, must be placed high up on shelves where only adults can reach. Every kitchen needs to be equipped with a fire extinguisher. Every floor of the house must be equipped with a smoke alarm. If you have firearms, they should be locked away in cabinets with the ammunition stored separately. The yard has to be fenc—"

"Cal?" Diana moaned his name. "Suddenly I'm not feeling well."

He took one look at his ashen-faced wife and his heart lurched. "Let's go."

In an instant he was out of his chair helping her to her feet. "Lean on me," he murmured. Throwing an arm around her, he walked her out of the room as swiftly as he could.

"I'm going to be sick."

"The rest room is right down here. Hold on."

With no thought of who might be inside, he pushed the door open and helped her to a stall. Drawing her hair back in his hand, he helped steady her while she lost her dinner.

They'd gone to a little Italian bistro around the corner from the social services complex. That was almost four hours ago. Maybe it was food poisoning, but if that were the case, Cal figured he would be sick by now, too.

"Better?" he asked when she'd completed an episode.

"Not really. I don't dare move."

"Then we won't."

While he supported her trembling weight, he wiped her mouth with tissue. Sure enough she was sick again.

A few minutes later, "All right now?" There couldn't be anything left in her stomach to lose.

"I—I don't feel as nauseated, but I'm so dizzy. Help me!" She clutched his arms. It was like déjà vu.

This could be a bad case of stomach flu, but Cal feared it might be related to her head injury. Not about to take any chances, he picked her up in his arms and carried her out of the building to the parking terrace.

Fortunately the hospital wasn't that far away. By the time they arrived at the emergency entrance Diana insisted she was feeling a little better and didn't need a doctor.

"Let's let someone examine you just to be sure. It's only been a month since your fall. I want to take every precaution."

She argued with him all the way inside. To his

relief, Dr. Farr, the same doctor who had treated her a month ago, was on duty and greeted Diana like an old friend. Cal explained the situation, grateful the other man knew Diana's history.

"Your husband was right to bring you in, Mrs. Rawlins. Let's get your vital signs. Then I'll call Dr. Harkness."

"I feel silly," she said after he'd taken her blood pressure and left the cubicle. "Oh, I hate it in here." Her voice shook.

"So do I." Cal practically groaned the words as he pulled up the stool next to her. "But we have a son who needs a healthy mother." *And I need you, my love.*

His eyes wandered hungrily over the lines and curves of her reclining figure. She'd always been perfect to him, from her golden hair to the creamy matte of her skin.

"I hope everything's all right at home with the baby. Annabelle must be wondering where we are." Her eyes were still closed.

"Not at all. I told her not to expect us before midnight."

"Why did you say that?"

"Because I thought we might enjoy a movie after class. You became ill before I could make the suggestion."

"I didn't realize. Forgive me for ruining your plans."

"Good grief, Diana!" he muttered angrily. "Why in the hell are you apologizing for getting sick?"

Her lids flew open. "I—I'm sorry. I didn't mean

to upset you again.'' Her green eyes pleaded with him for understanding. ''What I was trying to say is, I wish we could have gone.''

He heard a beseeching quality that told him she meant it. Appeased for the moment he said, ''So do I, but there will be other nights. Have you noticed how Annie jumps at the chance to baby-sit?''

''She confided to me that she wants a baby more than anything in the world.''

''So does Rand. They just need to give it a little more time. How's the dizziness now?''

''About the same.''

''As long as it's not worse.''

''It's not. Thank you for staying in here with me.''

He fought to control his anger once more. ''Where else would I be?''

''Nowhere else, because that's the kind of man you are.'' The tremor in her voice, the compliment she paid him, reminded him strongly of the old Diana. It had an immediate softening effect on him. ''Cal?''

''Yes?'' He had to clear his throat.

''I—I'm afraid. What if it's serious? The lady from social services is coming over next week to make her final inspection. If she finds out I'm too sick, she won't let us keep Tyler. I think I'd die if that happened. Don't let them take him away from me.'' Her plea bordered on panic.

''That's not going to happen, Diana,'' he vowed.

''You promise?''

''I swea—''

''Mrs. Rawlins?'' Dr. Farr chose that moment to pull the curtain aside so he could enter. ''Dr.

Harkness wants us to do some lab work. I'm afraid you'll have to leave us for a while, Mr. Rawlins.''

"Don't go far!" she cried out as Cal turned to go.

His heart knocked in its chest cavity. The behavior she was displaying right now was such a far cry from a month ago, he could scarcely credit it. "There's no chance of that. I'll be waiting for you in the lounge.''

After he reached the reception area, he phoned Annabelle with the news. Apparently Rand had joined her. They were ready and willing to tend the baby all night and tomorrow if necessary. Tyler was being his angelic self. Cal wasn't to worry about anything.

With heartfelt thanks to his friends he rang off, then wandered outside to get away from the hospital smell.

July had started out hot, ninety degrees. Though it was ten-thirty at night, the heat was still rising from the pavement. Cal loved summer. He could smell honeysuckle in the air. Everything was a reminder of Diana. The ache for her was growing more intense.

At this point in time he had just about reconciled himself to the probability that she would never get her memory back. But he couldn't handle it if something else were seriously wrong. *How would he live if anything happened to her?*

Several ambulances drove up with sirens blaring. They reminded him that she'd fallen just a few yards ahead of him. That fall had changed their lives irrevocably.

Not wanting to dwell on the painful past he hurried inside, anxious to find out what Dr. Farr had discovered. Diana wasn't in her cubicle. He sat in there and waited, growing more and more anxious.

Forty-five agonizing minutes passed. Then, "Mr. Rawlins? I'm glad you're here. Your wife will be back from the rest room shortly. This gives us time to talk alone."

Dr. Farr had said those same words to Cal a month ago. Something serious was wrong with Diana. He rose to his feet, filled with indescribable fear.

"Does this have to do with her head injury? Maybe she should have been kept in bed after I first took her home. If there are complications, I want the whole truth no matter how bad it is."

"Mr. Rawlins— There are complications, but not from the fall. Therefore we didn't have to resort to an X ray."

What?

"Tell me something. Has she remembered anything at all since the accident?"

"Other than Tyler's name, nothing."

"Then tell me something else. When was the last time you had sexual relations with your wife? This is important because according to her, she says you haven't slept together since you took her home from the hospital."

"That's right," Cal muttered, trying to figure out where this conversation was headed. "The last time we made love was the morning of her accident."

"That was almost five weeks ago."

"Yes."

"Did you use protection?"

"No. Even though the obstetrician urged Diana to give her body a rest after the last miscarriage, she wanted to keep trying for another baby."

''I see. Now the pieces of the puzzle have fallen into place.''

Cal grimaced. ''What puzzle?''

''Your wife's symptoms could mean that any number of things might be wrong with her. Before resorting to an X-ray, we wanted to make sure we'd covered all the bases, so we got a urine sample. The lab ran a test and it came out positive. She's pregnant.''

Pregnant—

The world reeled for a moment.

''My wife's pregnant?'' he whispered incredulously.

''That's right.''

Cal shook his head in disbelief. ''You're certain there can be no mistake about this?''

Dr. Farr smiled. ''I'd stake my license on it. She's in perfect health. You now have your explanation for the vomiting and dizziness.''

''We're going to have another baby. It's unbelievable.''

''Another one?''

''That's right. We took Baby Doe home with us. He'll be ours as soon as the adoption goes through.''

The doctor shook his head. ''I thought I'd seen everything in ER, but this is a new one for the books. Didn't your wife display these symptoms with her other pregnancies?''

''No. None.''

''Then I can see why you didn't consider pregnancy one of the reasons for her sick spell earlier tonight. Her morning sickness could be a good indication that she won't lose this one.''

Cal's heart beat faster. "Why do you say that?''

''It's just something I heard the chief of obstetrics tell the interns while we were on rotation. He admitted that it was an old wives' tale, but he warned that those old tales were inevitably true.''

The news kept getting better and better. ''Does Diana know?''

''Not yet. I wanted to talk to you first before I discussed her pregnancy with your OB. Because of her medical history, it's extremely important that he be informed immediately.''

''I couldn't agree more. It's Dr. Leo Brown.''

''He's a legend around here. Tell you what. You stay put and comfort your wife when she comes back, but say nothing to her. As soon as I've conferred with Dr. Harkness, I'll phone Dr. Brown. When I return, I'll have all the facts at hand. At that point you can tell your wife yourself.''

After offering his congratulations, Dr. Farr slipped out of the cubicle.

Cal stood there in a daze. His elation made it impossible to articulate his feelings. He and Diana already had their first son. Now she was expecting their second child. Two babies in one year. That settled it.

She couldn't leave him now.

''Hi,'' the orderly said a few minutes later as he wheeled Diana inside the cubicle and helped her to the table. When he left, it took all the self-control Cal could muster to not crush his wife in his arms and blurt out the fantastic news.

"How's the dizziness?" He struggled to keep his voice level as he urged her to lie down and relax.

"A little better since the nurse gave me some cola."

"That's a good sign you're going to be fine. Are you still nauseated?"

"I feel kind of queasy, but not nearly as dreadful as I did earlier." She glanced at her watch for the tenth time. "What do you think is taking the doctor so long?"

Her anguish would have torn him apart if he hadn't known the truth about her condition.

"You saw how busy the ER is tonight. The lab must be backed up with work."

"You're right, but it doesn't make the waiting any easier. I'm too impatient."

"Anyone would be."

"Do you think Tyler's okay?"

"Annie would have phoned me on my cellular if anything was wrong."

"You're right. I know I'm driving you cr—"

"Sorry this has taken so long," Dr. Farr announced as he swept into the cubicle. "The good news is, there's nothing wrong with you."

"You mean, I'm really all right?" The relief in her voice was tangible.

"I would say you're more than all right. Now your husband has permission to tell you why you were weren't feeling well earlier. Maybe it's a good thing you're lying down." But he grinned as he said it.

Her stunned gaze flew from the doctor to Cal. She

sat up on the table, her blond hair in breathtaking disarray. "You know why I got sick to my stomach?"

Suddenly Cal had difficulty swallowing. Once upon a time this news would have made her ecstatic. But that was before the accident. He had no idea how this was going to affect her now. "In about seven and a half months, you're going to give birth to our baby."

After a long silence, "I'm *pregnant?*" Shock had deepened her eyes to an intense green.

"The test was conclusive," Dr. Farr interjected.

"I know exactly how you feel," Cal rushed to reassure her. "It's just that I've had a little more time than you for the news to sink in."

"But we haven't—" She stopped midsentence, obviously embarrassed to be discussing anything so intimate in front of the doctor. A rosy blush stained her neck and cheeks.

Cal rubbed his chest absently. "We made love before you left the house on the morning of your accident. That had to be the date of your conception because it was the only time we didn't use protection since your last miscarriage.

"Dr. Brown, your obstetrician, had warned us not to get pregnant again too soon. But after three months you were so afraid you might have trouble conceiving, we decided to forgo protection and let nature take its course."

Her eyes rounded in stunned surprise. The revelations were coming too hard and fast for her to absorb. He couldn't tell if she were happy with the news or not. It was the not knowing that gave him the enormous pit in his stomach.

"Mrs. Rawlins? I've already spoken with Dr. Brown. He wants to see you in his office tomorrow. You're to call his receptionist after eight in the morning for an appointment. She'll fit you in."

"Thank you, Dr. Farr," she whispered, still sounding dazed.

"You're welcome. If you want my personal opinion, for what it's worth," he added gently, "you're lucky to be pregnant now. At first it will be difficult dealing with two babies so close together. Sometimes you think you'll lose your mind. I ought to know.

"My wife and I had twins while I was in undergraduate school. But it was worth it. Now that they're older, they have each other to play with all the time. It's a blessing in disguise."

"I—I'm sure you're right. Thank you, Doctor."

"You bet. Now I'll leave you two alone."

"I'll be right back, Diana."

Cal followed the doctor out of the cubicle. "Thank you for everything," he said in a low aside. "I'm glad you were here for Diana on both occasions. You handled everything just right."

"It's my job."

"You do it well, believe me."

"So do you, Mr. Rawlins. Despite her memory loss I can tell your wife has already grown more comfortable around you during the last month."

Comfortable maybe. But nothing else...

"I don't think I could handle it if mine didn't know me, didn't remember our life together. You're both very courageous. Good luck."

* * *

It had only taken a second to get fully dressed, but Diana waited until she could see the doctor walk away from Cal before she left the cubicle. The way the two of them had their heads together, she was fairly certain they wouldn't like their private conversation interrupted. Especially not her husband.

He'd taken the news about her pregnancy too calmly. That enigmatic veneer he displayed on occasion masked the flesh and blood man beneath. Though he would deny it to his dying breath because it was the way he was made, with one baby at home and another one on the way, the real Cal probably felt more trapped than ever. No doubt he was bearing his soul to the doctor.

It had been five weeks since the accident. She'd already had two sessions with Dr. Beal who'd talked her through her initial fears and seemed pleased that both she and Cal were working in harmony at building a new marriage.

He'd advised her to face each day as if the glass were half full, instead of half empty. Up to now that philosophy had worked pretty well. Certainly Cal had been the model father and husband.

Who else would have stood in the bathroom and held his wife while she was sick? As far as Diana was concerned, he was perfect in all departments. Everyone praised him, especially Dr. Beal.

But their marriage was far from perfect. In the strictest sense of the term, they didn't have one. *Except on paper.*

Cal never sought her company unless it had to do with Tyler. He hadn't once tried to get things on a more personal level. A little while ago in the cubicle when she'd been so frightened, she'd secretly hoped he would reach for her hand. She yearned for his touch. Nothing...

No, that wasn't exactly true. He had planned to take her to a movie tonight. Naturally he felt like he needed a breather. After being cooped up with her and the baby most of the time, who could blame him? What better place than a public theater where nothing personal would be expected of him.

Instead, they'd ended up in emergency because of her. *Always because of her.* Now a new lifetime responsibility had been placed on Cal's shoulders.

How often since that first night at the hospital had he regretted the things he'd said to her because he'd been so certain her memory would come back?

Let's get something straight, Diana. This is no sacrifice for me. You're my wife. I'm in love with you. I want you in all the ways a man can want a woman. I would do anything to keep you in my life.

Tears stung her eyes because the miracle hadn't happened. The man who'd so bravely stated his undying love no longer existed. In his place stood a magnificent facsimile who would act the part and do his duty for God and man come hell or high water.

If she hadn't gone over the edge because of Tyler, if she hadn't been so damned selfish, none of this would have happened. Cal wouldn't be condemned to live in a marriage with a woman he would never choose of his own free will if he had it to do over again.

She should have followed her basic instincts that

first day. Cal said he would have agreed to a separation. She knew he would have helped her find an apartment. They could have filed for an amicable divorce. Later on, when she discovered she was pregnant, he would have worked out visitation arrangements with her once the baby was born. Thousands of other couples handled similar situations in the same manner. It wasn't impossible.

But no. Her wants, her needs superseded his. Afraid she was on the verge of a psychotic break, her husband had been forced to move heaven and earth so they could end up taking Tyler home.

Was it any wonder Cal only ever truly acted happy around the baby or other people who dropped over? He carried his burden like a mantle, but when Roman or his other friends were present, a subtle transition occurred and he would discard it for a while.

During those moments she saw the animation light up his eyes. Sometimes in the evenings Rand or Gerard would drive up in front while Cal was outside doing yard work. They'd enjoy a beer together on the lawn as they must have done on countless other occasions.

Cal's deep-throated laughter would drift through the open French doors to thrill her. But those were facets of his personality he never showed around her.

Because he doesn't desire you, Diana. Face it. You've changed, and there's no way you can go back to the woman he fell in love with. More than any man, her husband deserved his freedom. She saw the way other women acted around him. Sometimes she wanted to scratch their eyes out for staring at him, especially the flashy brunette in their night class. *Veronica.*

Diana had no way of knowing if she'd been a jealous wife before the accident, but she recognized that destructive trait in herself now.

It was a good thing the classes were over or she might have said something to the other woman like, "If you don't stop making a spectacle of yourself around my husband, *Veronica,* I'll have to tell the social worker you're not a fit foster parent."

Every time she remembered how that woman fell all over herself to get Cal's attention, Diana felt a surge of adrenaline attack her body.

Her jealousy wasn't something she was proud of. She would never have admitted it to Dr. Beal. Besides, she didn't want to hear him explain the facts of the situation. She already knew them by heart.

Number one, Cal wasn't in love with her, which made her defensive and vulnerable. Number two, he could have any woman he wanted. Though to his credit, he always acted like they didn't exist. Number three, she'd come to realize he was by far the most attractive man she had ever met or known. If the truth be known, she could parrot his words with one minor change. *I want you, Cal Rawlins, in all the ways a woman can want a man.*

Looking back to that first day, it didn't seem possible she'd pushed him away. *You should have kept pushing, Diana.*

Divorce was their only answer.

She would broach the subject tonight before they went to their separate beds. But if she did that, they'd both lose Tyler. Their dear sweet, precious baby. How could she let him go? How could Cal?

You're being selfish again. You say you love that child so much? Then prove it and give him up. If his birth mother could do it to ensure him a better life, then so can you.

Tyler deserved to be raised by two people madly in love with each other. Only *that* kind of love would spill over to an innocent baby who asked only to be loved and made to feel secure by a mother and father living under the same roof.

The baby growing inside of her deserved both parents living under the same roof, as well. But the accident had changed the course of their lives forever. Diana had to do what was best for Tyler *and* her husband.

As for their unborn child, provided she could stay pregnant the full nine months, it would be better for him or her to grow up in a home without tension.

She couldn't promise that, not if she stayed with Cal. Nothing could be worse than wanting a man who no longer wanted you. The pain had already begun. Her baby might already have picked up on her anxiety in that uncanny way an unborn child was purported to do.

No. There could only be one answer. She had to go her own way alone. After the baby was born, she would lavish all her affection on it. So would Cal. They'd just do it separately.

She refused to think about the woman who might be in Cal's future by then.

Armoring herself for what lay ahead, she put her

shoulders back and walked up behind Cal. "I'm ready to leave if you are."

He turned in the direction of her voice. His shuttered brown gaze made a thorough inventory of her face and figure.

Her heart might have gone into cardiac arrest if she hadn't known he was looking for physical signs that he'd impregnated her. Even more important, he was wondering if she'd be sick in the car before they made it home.

"I feel much better since I drank the rest of the Coke," she assured him before he could ask the question hovering on those compelling male lips she'd longed to feel against hers for some time now.

"I'm glad," came the quiet reply. "Let's get you home to bed. Just so you know, I'll be taking care of Tyler during the night from now on."

Like the devoted husband he'd already proved to be, Cal's mind had been working overtime. He'd braced himself to handle whatever life had ready to deal out. His valiance under the uniqueness of their domestic crisis had to be unequaled.

Diana chose not to argue with him. She would bide her time until they'd arrived home and had said their good-nights to the Dunbartons. Provided Tyler was asleep, then she would ask Cal to join her in the living room for a talk.

"You're quiet tonight," he murmured as they drove toward the freeway.

So are you, Cal, and we both know why.

"Has the nausea come back?"

"No." She rolled down the window and breathed

the fragrant night air. For the first time since she'd known him, she felt self-conscious around him because her mind was entertaining thoughts which she knew were far removed from his. "Tell me about Dr. Brown, is it? Do I like him?"

"Very much," he finally answered her, but his voice sounded strange.

"Is he young, old?"

"Middle-aged. Kind to a fault."

"That's nice to hear. I'm relieved."

"*Diana*—" Her name hung precariously in the air. "Talk to me, dammit! Tell me what's going on inside you. We've just been told you're pregnant. It's the most important news two parents can hear who've wanted a baby as much as we have."

For once, the veneer had worn thin.

She took a fortifying breath. "I agree. Actually there's a lot I have to say. It will probably take some time. Since we're almost home, why don't we put off talking until Rand and Annabelle have gone. Is that okay with you?"

All she heard in response was the sound of the radial tires whirring against the pavement as the Saab picked up speed.

CHAPTER EIGHT

"GOOD night, you two. Thanks again for watching Tyler."

"Anytime. You know that."

Cal stood in the middle of the living room eyeing his wife who'd gone to the foyer with Rand and Annabelle. When they'd asked what had happened at the hospital, she'd glossed over the experience as nothing more than food poisoning.

Not a word about her pregnancy.

Diana hadn't been herself since learning the news. The change in her added a new dimension to their relationship. He didn't trust the undercurrents crackling between them.

Bless little Tyler who lay sound asleep in his crib. She couldn't use him as a shield to put off their talk. In the car she'd said they *were* going to talk. Prophetic words since he'd been planning to have an intimate discussion with her for quite some time now.

He'd hoped a movie would relax her before he told her the separate sleeping arrangements weren't working out. He needed her. If she couldn't remember what it felt like to make love, then he would help her to remember.

Even if they didn't touch, they could at least start sharing the same bed. When she felt comfortable enough with him, then he would hold her, kiss her, nothing more if she didn't want it.

Diana might have been a virgin when he'd married her. But on their wedding night they'd both been so on fire for each other, her natural instincts had taken over. From the very beginning their lovemaking had always been a mutually satisfying experience.

This time he would be gentle and loving until she was ready for more. If he promised to let her set the pace, then she wouldn't have to be afraid. He knew she trusted him. Deep in his gut he felt reasonably confident that her initial repulsion of him had disappeared. It was a beginning. He wanted that beginning to start tonight.

"Cal? They've gone."

Finally.

Every time she entered a room on those long, shapely legs of hers, his heart turned over. Her softly rounded figure in the silky white summer dress had never looked more appealing. Pregnancy gave her a subtle radiance he found irresistible.

He studied the classic features of her lovely face. The combination of golden hair and green eyes always took his breath.

If she felt uncomfortable with him staring at her, and apparently she did if her crimson cheeks were anything to go by, then maybe that wasn't such a bad thing. She needed to realize he was a man with wants and desires who enjoyed looking at his beautiful wife.

Since the accident, if they had to be in the living room together, she normally curled up at the far end of the couch, almost defying him to come closer.

Tonight she remained standing, as if to garner additional strength. Why?

His hands went to his hips. "It seems we both have a lot on our minds. Why don't you tell me what's bothering you first?"

She was nervous. He could tell by the way she folded her arms against her waist.

"All right," she said in a shaky tone. "I think it would be best if we divorced right away."

He froze in place. Surely he hadn't heard her correctly.

"Say that again?" he demanded quietly.

She averted her eyes. "I know this has come as a shock, but it's—"

"Shock doesn't begin to cover it," he cut her off brutally. "Less than an hour ago we learned that we're going to have a baby. How in God's name can you talk about divorce in the same breath?"

He'd known anger before, but never like this. "What are you planning to do? Forgo the surgical procedure to ensure that you miscarry again?"

"No, Cal— You've got to listen to me!"

"Why?" he bit out. "So I can hear what scheme you've concocted to get rid of Tyler, too?"

Her head flew back to reveal a blanched face washed in tears. "You don't understand. Giving up Tyler is going to be the hardest thing I've ever had to do, but he deserves a home with two parents who love each other."

"And we don't, is that it?" The dagger had found its mark.

"Please, Cal— Just this once let's be honest. I'm not the same woman you married."

"Have I ever once complained about that?"

She started to back away from him and ended up bumping into the couch. "No. Because the Cal Rawlins I've been living with is too honorable a man to push his wife away, even if she's a stranger to him."

"You're hardly a stranger."

"You know what I mean." Her voice trembled.

"No. I'm afraid you're going to have to tell me."

He saw her hand go to her throat in another nervous gesture. "I know I'm very different from the person I used to be. All our friends have been so wonderful to me, but at unguarded moments I see their eyes watching me. L-like I'm a freak."

Her vulnerability tugged at his heart, dissipating some of his rage. "Have I made you feel like one, too?"

"No!" came her emphatic avowal. He supposed he should be thankful for that much. "That's the problem."

"*What's* the problem?"

"You never react or show what you're really thinking, not like the others. But I know deep down in my soul that you're constantly making comparisons."

Cal raked a hand through his hair. "You mean you *want* me to tell you all the ways you've changed since the accident?"

"Yes! N-no— Oh, I don't know. Either way, it doesn't matter, does it?" she cried in anguish. "I'm not the same person."

"No. You're not."

"When you told me at the hospital that you loved me, that's because you never dreamed I'd still have amnesia five weeks later."

"You're wrong, Diana. The first time you pushed me away and wouldn't kiss me back, I had the strongest premonition that your memory would never return. To be honest, I haven't operated on that hope since I brought you home from the hospital with Tyler."

Those words seemed to drain her energy. He watched her sink back against the pillows of the couch. "I don't know why, but I don't think it's going to come back, either."

Her plaintive tone tore him to pieces.

"Sometimes I've almost gone crazy trying to pretend that it doesn't matter. Other days I've lived in denial that the accident ever happened. But then I look at pictures around the house. My parents and grandparents, your parents and grandparents, our wedding, our trips, our friends. Nothing's familiar to me. Absolutely nothing. You can't imagine how strange it is."

For the first time since the accident, she was letting him inside. He needed to hear it all.

Getting down on his haunches in front of her he said, "Tell me what it's like."

"It's awful. The other day I was watching television when this woman came on the program who'd had an out-of-body experience. She had died on the operating table, but she felt herself rise above her body and look down at it.

"That's exactly how I felt when Brittany showed

me a video of one of the Christmas parties you and I hosted at our other house.''

A shudder racked his body. ''She should have known better.'' He'd purposely kept their videos out of sight for that very reason.

''Don't blame her, Cal. My curiosity grew so acute I pretty well forced her to let me watch it. Just once I wanted to see the way you and I reacted to each other before my accident.''

''Which film did you look at?''

''The one last Christmas where you were playing the violin and I was accompanying you on the piano. It was 'O Holy Night.' I had no idea we shared a love of music....''

His eyes closed. At the end of the piece he'd leaned down to give her a kiss that went on and on. As long as Roman was making movies, Cal decided he wanted to preserve their kiss for posterity. At that point in time Diana was pregnant. Since she knew they were being filmed, she cooperated with a passionate response that brought a hearty round of applause from everyone.

He cleared his throat. ''We used to perform at church on occasion.''

''Brittany told me,'' she admitted quietly. ''How come I haven't seen your violin?''

''It needed to be restrung. I just haven't bothered to pick it up yet.''

Her stillness haunted him.

''The other day after I'd put Tyler down for his nap,'' she began, ''I got some sheet music out of the piano bench and sat down to see if I could play. I sat there, and sat there.'' Her voice shook.

He waited. At first there was silence, then he heard her muffled sobs.

''I can't let you stay married to me, Cal, but I swear you'll be able to share equally in the raising of our child after it's born. As for T-Tyler—'' She couldn't go on.

Slowly he rose to his feet and stared down at her. He was about to take a risk that could lose him everything. But considering that the alternative meant he'd already lost, he might as well go down fighting.

''If that's the way you really feel, then I'll give you a divorce. We'll start proceedings this week if you like. But first, you have to do something for me tonight.''

She lifted her head. ''What is it?''

''Come to bed with me.''

In some perverse way her gasp pleased him. She'd turned his world upside down with her talk of divorce. Now the shoe was on the other foot.

''I won't do anything you don't want me to. I just want to feel you next to me until we both fall asleep. Your accident tore you abruptly away from me. Tonight will give me the opportunity to say a proper goodbye to my wife.

''It's been a long time since I held you.'' His voice throbbed. ''In the dark I won't know the difference between the new and the old Diana. Your scent is the same. Your skin and hair are the same. For once I won't be making comparisons.''

He turned to leave. ''If you don't join me after

you've given Tyler a bottle, then I'll know it was too much to ask in return for your freedom.''

Diana left Tyler's room at ten after two, then hurried to the guest bathroom for a shower. After slipping on one of her old nightgowns she hadn't worn before, she tiptoed past the nursery to the master bedroom. Her husband had invited her to his bed. She intended to join him.

His comment about not knowing which Diana he held in the dark gave her the courage to act on her desire. She could never let it show that she had fallen in love with him. He would be shocked if he knew how much she wanted to be close to him.

What a cruel irony that she remembered nothing of their baby's conception. But as long as she was going to have his child, she wanted a memory of lying in his arms for the rest of the night. It would have to last her a lifetime.

''Diana?''

She jumped. ''Please don't turn on the light.''

''I wasn't going to. I simply wanted you to know I hadn't gone to sleep.''

Her heart gave an extra beat. She might have found it easier if he hadn't been awake. There was enough light from the July moon that she could see his reclining silhouette. It made him look bigger somehow. She'd thought she could do this, but now that the opportunity presented itself, she wasn't so sure.

''Don't run away.'' He could read her mind. It was humiliating.

''I—I'm not.''

"I'll close my eyes if it will help."

"*It won't,*" she said before she realized the ridiculousness of the situation.

"I might snarl once in a while, but I don't bite."

Her mouth turned up at the corners before she found the temerity to take the last few steps to reach the bed. After climbing in on her side, she pulled up the covers. "You don't snarl."

"How do you know?"

"Because I've never heard you."

"So you were listening. I'll take that as a compliment."

Heat suffused her face. She could be thankful for the darkness. "With Tyler in the house, I've developed a keen sense of hearing."

"Haven't we all."

She smiled again. "I think you must be unusual."

"In what way?" He had turned on his side to face her. Even though several inches separated them, she could feel the warmth from his body.

"Brittany told me that after the first week, Roman slept through Yuri's night feedings."

"I'm not surprised. The nature of his work often demands he turn his days and nights around. He has to grab sleep when he can."

"It makes me feel guiltier than ever that we stayed over there after we brought Tyler home from the hospital."

He raised up on his elbow, taking part of the covers with him. "Roman would have been mortally offended if we'd gone anywhere else. Besides, he lived with us for a couple of weeks when his house was being remodeled.''

She didn't know that. ''Before he married Brittany?''

''That's right. He's been looking for a way to pay us back ever since.''

''Then I feel a little better about it.''

''Better enough to come closer?''

Suddenly he slid his arm beneath her head and drew her toward him. She had no choice but to roll into him and bury her face in his neck.

They seemed to fit perfectly together. Through every day living, she'd unintentionally caught sight of him in various stages of undress. But the reality of lying against his powerful body came as a revelation, especially his rock-hard legs entwined with hers.

He'd put on a T-shirt and sweats. His skin smelled of the clean lemony soap he used. With a sense of wonderment she heard a deep groan escape his throat, almost as if he'd been running for a very long time and had finally come to the end of his journey.

When he kissed her hair, she started to tremble. He must have felt her response because his free hand splayed across her back, gentling her like he might a little filly.

''Am I frightening you?'' His low, vibrant voice sent delicious chills racing up and down her body.

''No.''

''Then why are you shivering. Are you cold?''

Lying in his arms like this was like standing too close to a bonfire. ''You know I'm not,'' she blurted.

She felt his enticing chuckle to the marrow of her bones. "I love this new honesty of yours."

Her breath caught. "You mean I wasn't honest before?"

"You were, but since the accident you wear it like a banner. It presents all kinds of exciting new challenges. Keeps me on my feet. There's no chance of our marriage going stale."

Stale? Had he forgotten they were getting a divorce?

"I had no idea I was so entertaining," came her grumpy retort.

"You're a great deal more than that." He kissed the side of her neck. Her heart began to pound unmercifully. "You've become a woman of mystery. I never know what to expect next. When I married you, I never dreamed I was going to get two wives for the price of one."

"I thought you said you wouldn't be able to tell the difference between us in the dark."

He laughed so hard the bed shook. She loved the sound of it. "I lied."

"Your honesty is rather shocking itself."

"Would you prefer it if I didn't tell the truth?"

"No," she half moaned. "That would be horrible."

"I agree. No matter what the future brings, we know we have that going for us."

She stirred restlessly. Without realizing it, her hand had moved up his chest. She felt him suck in his breath and stilled her fingers immediately.

"Can we talk about it?"

"About what?"

"The future."

"We can talk about whatever you want," he whispered against the soft skin of her cheek. When he gently grazed her earlobe with his teeth, it did more shocking things to her nervous system. "The only problem is, it's after three and I have an early morning staff meeting at the office."

Her spirits plummeted. "I didn't realize."

"That's because I forgot to mention it. When you became ill earlier tonight, everything went out of my head. But I tell you what. Though I might not be able to stay awake the whole time, I'll promise to try."

Guilt consumed her. "No, Cal. Our talk can wait."

"You're sure?"

"Positive. You need your sleep. Shall I wake you when I get up for Tyler at six-thirty?"

"That would be perfect. Good night, Diana."

"Good night."

She started to get out of bed but his arms tightened around her. "Don't move. You're right where I want you."

When she least expected it, he leaned across to plant a kiss on her parted lips. "In case you were worried, I plan to keep the meeting short. That way I can be ready to drive you and Tyler to Dr. Brown's for your appointment whenever you say. All you have to do is call me on the cellular."

She could scarcely breathe with his mouth this close to hers. "I'd hate to disturb you during a meeting."

"You used to disturb me a lot. It made my day. I

couldn't wait to get home every night to my beautiful wife. All the men at the office were jealous, especially when you would drop over on your lunch hour to give me a quickie.''

Her eyes rounded. "A *quickie?*"

"Hmm. A kiss with the promise of things to come. Roman used to tease you mercilessly about it. It goes something like this."

His mouth descended, claiming hers with a possessiveness that left her drowning in sensation. When he deepened their kiss, it felt like a lightning bolt had charged every cell in her body.

"*That,* is a quickie."

She could have cried aloud when he relinquished her lips and settled back against the pillows. She hadn't wanted him to stop. What made it worse was that within minutes, he was making sounds which meant he had succumbed to the exhaustion racking his body. She, on the other hand, had never been more wide awake!

Because of her accident, his whole life had changed in the last five weeks. A new house, a new baby.

A new wife.

Another baby on the way.

He'd done the tasks of a dozen men to accommodate her. No doubt her needs had driven him to the breaking point.

According to Brittany, Cal wasn't just another Realtor. At an early age he had become a savvy property investor and developer. Today he enjoyed the reputation of being one of the most prominent businessmen in the Salt Lake Valley.

It humbled her to realize that with all the load of responsibility he carried on his shoulders, he'd still been able to take care of her and the baby nonstop without complaint. Divorcing him would throw his world into even greater chaos. But she refused to stand in the way of his right to choose the woman he wanted to live with for the rest of his life.

Because of Tyler, the divorce needed to be dealt with immediately. Their adorable baby's welfare took top priority over any other considerations. Every day they parented him, they were endangering his ability to bond emotionally with his adoptive parents. The sooner social services found him a home, the better.

But she felt a sick pain whenever she contemplated a permanent separation from either Tyler or Cal. They had become her whole life! One of them was safe asleep in the nursery. The other was safe asleep in her arms. But it was all a dream that would vanish in daylight.

Insisting that Tyler come home from the hospital with them was a big mistake. Almost as big a one as getting into bed with her husband.

You wanted a memory, Diana.

You have it.

You've just experienced a kiss from your husband and it's not enough. You want more.

You want it all.

You're never going to be the same again.

Dr. Brown's reception room remained crowded no matter how many pregnant women with children in hand, came in or out of his office. Cal didn't feel the least bit out of place with Tyler propped against his shoulder.

Diana had dressed him in a little baseball suit with baby tennis shoes and a matching baseball cap. Cal turned it around so the rim hung down at the back of his neck. Everyone from the receptionist to the children wanted to hold his cute baby boy who looked just like him.

Cal couldn't have felt more like Tyler's father if Tyler had been the son of his own body. No matter what Diana said, there was no way he was going to lose this little guy or let her walk out of his life.

Last night her response to his kiss had almost given him a heart attack. Her mind might not remember their old life together, but her body had recognized him. Physically she'd been ready for him. In fact she had reacted so much like his loving, giving Diana, he'd almost forgotten there'd ever been an accident. After five weeks' deprivation, it took all his restraint not to make love to her in earnest. But at the crucial moment, he came to his senses knowing it would have been a grave mistake. She was still fighting him mentally.

He shifted their sleepy son to his other shoulder.

The mind was a powerful thing. In order to make her realize she was in love with him, he had to do something drastic.

Last night when she'd told him she wanted a divorce, his mind had devised another plan. It was probably more immoral and illegal than the one he'd come up with to get her and the baby to go home with him from the hospital the first time.

The excuse he'd given Diana about having an early morning meeting with his staff had been a partial lie. He did have a meeting, but he'd made it with Whitney while Diana had been giving Tyler his midnight bottle.

This morning he'd driven to her law firm. She welcomed him inside and listened to his ideas. To his intense relief, she had gone along with them. She even applauded them because she loved Diana and wanted to help him fight for his wife and children.

"Mr. Rawlins? Dr. Brown would like to talk to you in his office."

At the sound of the nurse's voice he got to his feet and carried Tyler through the reception area and down the hall to the doctor's private office.

"Dr. Brown." He nodded before he placed Tyler in Diana's outstretched arms, then took a chair next to his wife opposite the doctor's desk.

Their middle-aged obstetrician beamed at Cal. "Double congratulations to you both."

"Thank you, Dr. Brown. It's a lot to absorb but I'm not complaining. How is my wife?"

"Generally speaking, she's in excellent health. Her iron is a little low, but I'll give her pills for that along with the prenatal vitamins and a new drug to help her with the nausea.

"I've just been explaining to her that we need to do the procedure to close the uterus as soon as possible. It can be done right here in my office day after tomorrow. Though it will only require a localized anesthetic, she'll need someone to lean on when she walks out of here afterwards. I'd like to start early.

Seven a.m., which means you should be here by six-thirty.''

Cal turned to his wife who was busy kissing Tyler on the neck. ''Does that sound okay to you, Diana?''

She lifted her head but wouldn't look him in the eye. ''Yes, if it's all right with you. I didn't know your work schedule.''

''No problem.''

''Good.'' The doctor got to his feet and shook Cal's hand. ''Congratulations again.''

''Thank you.''

Cal put his arm around her waist to guide her from the office suite. He experienced a sense of family pride that grew more acute as the four of them proceeded down the hall toward the main entrance of the building. Every so often her hip brushed against his leg. After tasting her mouth last night, any contact electrified him.

Once they reached the parking terrace, he helped Diana into the car, then opened the rear door of the Saab and strapped Tyler in the infant seat. After plopping a pacifier in his mouth, he shut the door and went around to the driver's seat.

Before starting the motor he turned to her with a prayer in his heart that he was doing the right thing. ''Did you tell him we're getting a divorce?''

Her face suddenly lost all expression. She refused to look at him. ''No. I didn't think it was anyone's business but ours.''

''Except for our attorney, of course.''

The knuckles of her fingers looked a pinched white where her hand clawed the armrest.

Pleased with that much response he decided it was time to go for the jugular.

"Knowing how anxious you are to get started with the proceedings, I asked Whitney if she would handle it, and she agreed. She's a favorite of yours. I hope I did the right thing."

Her breathing sounded shallow. "You always do the right thing. I like her very much."

"Since it's a noncontested divorce, she can represent both of us without problem. She'll be discreet."

"I'm sure she will," he heard her say in such a quiet, defeated tone of voice, he didn't know if he could keep this up. But it was too late now and he was in too deep not to follow through, no matter the outcome.

"She says we need to give up Tyler immediately." A groan came from Diana's side of the car. "A colleague of hers in another office who handles adoptions on a regular basis has several sets of clients who've been through the legal process and are waiting for a baby. All she has to do is pick up the phone and Tyler can be permanently placed with a family as soon as tonight."

Dead silence met his remark.

"I like that idea much better than his having to go through a foster home first. Don't you?"

Her head was bowed. She couldn't speak.

I know I'm torturing you, darling, but I'll do whatever it takes to make you see what is right in front of your eyes if only you'll look.

"At least we can draw comfort from the fact that

we were his only foster parents, that we gave him all the love we knew how to give.''

Her shoulders were shaking.

''To save us going downtown, Whitney said she'd come by the house today on her lunch hour to get the paperwork started. It's possible that by this evening, the adoptive couple will want to pick him up.

''Since you're going in for minor surgery the day after tomorrow, this is probably the best way to handle everything. When you come home, you won't have to lift a finger.''

Dear Lord. Forgive me.

He made it obvious that he was looking at his watch, then shoved the key in the ignition. ''We'd better hurry home. After putting her other cases aside to help us, I'd hate to keep Whitney waiting.''

Bless you. Whitney, for going through this masquerade with me. If it doesn't work, then all our efforts will be made legal and binding. But I have to pray Diana will break down and admit she doesn't want a divorce before things get to that point.

CHAPTER NINE

"DIANA? What grounds do you want me to fill in here for your divorce?"

The three of them sat in the living room around the coffee table. As usual, Diana's husband had been the one with enough presence of mind to make sandwiches and supply drinks, but she noticed that Whitney was the only one to display an appetite.

Hugging Tyler closer to her chest, Diana darted her husband a covert glance. He hadn't said another word once they'd started home in the car from the clinic. The thought of their baby being taken away by as early as tonight was killing him, too. He looked gray around the mouth. *Dear God.*

"I realize this isn't a typical divorce, but I have to state a reason," Whitney said in an understanding tone. "Since you're the one initiating the proceedings, it should come from you."

Diana didn't know if she could go through with this while Cal was in the room. She kissed the top of the baby's head, savoring the sweet smell of baby powder on his skin. Whitney must have felt the tension in the room because she said, "Cal? Would you mind leaving us alone for a few minutes?"

"Not at all." His solemn expression crucified Diana. "Shall I take the baby?"

Much as she didn't want to give up Tyler, not even for an instant, she recognized that Cal was in pain.

With a nod she said, "That might be best. Give Mommy another kiss before you go."

Oh, Tyler, my darling boy.

She struggled not to break down in front of Cal as he lifted Tyler from her arms and strode across the living room toward the hall. But the second he disappeared around the corner, Diana found herself sobbing.

"This has to be horrible for both of you, Diana. I'm so sorry."

Five minutes later Diana had barely gotten herself under control. "Forgive me, Whitney."

"Take as long as you want. I told my paralegal I wouldn't be back in the office for the rest of the day. When I leave here, I'm going to see John Warren, the adoption attorney Cal told you about. He's a good friend.

"After being in this business for a while, it's his opinion that when you're dealing with a baby, it's best to do things quickly. It cuts down on the pain for everyone."

Diana groaned. "I thought I knew what pain was until Cal brought up the divorce in the car."

"He said the same thing when he told me you had asked him for a divorce. It's one thing to believe in what you're doing, but quite another to actually carry it out. I ought to know."

"What do you mean?"

"I never told you how I met Gerard, did I?"

"Only that you were on a European tour together."

"Yes, but you don't know why I was there. It's a long story. To make it short, let's just say my sister got pregnant on the same tour the year before. The man was married, but he had no conscience and ended up sleeping with her.

"I was so angry, I decided to track him down and throw the book at him so he'd have to face my sister in court and pay child support.

"In the beginning I was so driven by revenge, I didn't think about the ramifications of exposing him. I didn't consider how it might affect my sister or my innocent little nephew who had no control over his birth, or our family.

"Gerard had gone undercover on that tour to capture a known spy trading classified secrets to a foreign power. The lowlife turned out to be my sister's French teacher who used his students to help pass information. On that tour, he chose her for his target and made her pregnant. On my tour, he chose *me*."

"How horrible."

"You can say that again. Fortunately I had Gerard there to protect me. When I realized who the father really was, everything changed. I no longer wanted revenge, and I could understand why my sister didn't want anyone to know who the father was. I had been so certain I was doing the right thing for everyone. Instead, I almost ruined her life and my own."

"So your sister still has no idea that you know the identity of the father?"

"No. The family thought I went to Mexico and met Gerard there." She let out a deep sigh. "My point in telling you all this is that sometimes we start out thinking that we know exactly what we're doing. We think it's right for everyone, so we plunge ahead. The problem is, sometimes we're wrong. I was lucky to come to my senses before I did something I'd regret.

"As your attorney, I'm advising you to be very sure you want to divorce Cal and give up Tyler. It may seem the right thing to do this very minut—"

"He doesn't love me," Diana cried in anguish.

Whitney cocked her head. "He told me he *did.*"

She jumped to her feet and started pacing. "He just said that because he's so noble. Cal's not the kind of man to go back on a commitment as binding as marriage, even if his wife is psychotic!" Her voice throbbed.

Ignoring her outburst Whitney said quietly, "You've grown to love him, haven't you? Isn't that why you can't come up with a reason for divorcing him?"

"Yes, but I'm not the same woman he married."

"He knows that a lot better than you do, yet he wants to stay in the marriage."

She buried her face in her hands. "It's because of Tyler."

"If that's true, then give Tyler up and postpone the divorce. See what happens."

Diana's head reared back. "You don't understand. I'm pregnant."

"I know. Cal told me. I think it's wonderful."

"So do I, but don't you see? Having another baby just makes Cal feel that much more obligated to stay with me."

There was a long silence.

"I can see your mind is made up. You remind me of myself when I started out on that tour. All I can do is hope and pray that you won't live to regret it. Naturally I'll carry out your wishes."

"I—I don't have another choice, Whitney. Surely you can see that."

"It doesn't matter what I can see. You're the one who has to live with yourself and the ramifications of those actions. I'm going to put 'incompatibility due to amnesia on the part of the plaintiff' as the reason for the divorce.

"Cal has already set things up so that whether or not you go to work, you'll be financially secure for the rest of your life.

"He has properties throughout the valley and has stipulated that you may choose a home or a condo for you and the baby. He'll pay for any remodeling, decorating, and will furnish you a complete nursery with everything you need for the new baby.

"The court decides visitation so that it's fair to both mother and father. Cal told me to tell you he'll always pay for your medical and dent—"

"Please don't say any more," she cut in on her friend because she had started to feel sick. "I'm sorry. I don't mean to sound rude. My n-nausea seems to have come back."

"I heard you had morning sickness this time. I'm sorry. It's all you need on top of everything else."

"Whitney?" she blurted in alarm. "Cal said the adoptive parents might come tonight. The way I'm feeling, I couldn't possibly deal with people until tomorrow. Would that be all right?"

"It is on my part. But if John has already contacted his clients and made arrangements, then you might not have a choice."

"But how do we know they'll be the right parents for Tyler?"

"You don't. The only assurance you have is that they've been screened, their backgrounds have been checked and their homes have passed inspection."

Diana trembled. "The birth mother wanted me and Cal to raise him. She knew all about us. We were supposed to take him to church."

"I know. It would probably hurt her if she knew you had to give him up. But at the time, she could have no way of knowing you would want to divorce your husband."

"I don't want to, Whitney. I *have* to for his happiness."

"I understand. As soon as the papers are drawn up, I'll bring them over for your signatures." She got up from the love seat. "I'll hear from John later in the day and call you so you'll know what's happening." She put her arms around Diana and they clung.

"I'm sorry you and Cal are in so much pain. You know I'll do everything in my power to make this as easy as possible for you. If I can put John off until tomorrow, I will."

Diana mumbled her thanks before she ran blindly from the room to her bedroom where she could shut the door and cry out her despair in private.

At some point she must have fallen asleep because the next time she became aware of her surroundings, she could feel the baby's warm little body moving next to her. She let out a small cry and lifted her head from the pillow to discover that Cal and Tyler had joined her.

Her husband's beautiful dark brown eyes watched her, as if he were trying to find entrance to her soul. "We heard you crying earlier and came in to make you feel better."

Tyler lay between them wide awake. It felt so right, the three of them together. She reached over to kiss his dimpled cheek. The thought of never being able to do that again was too terrible to contemplate.

"Diana—" Cal murmured, "Whitney called to tell us she got hold of John. He has put his clients off until tomorrow."

"Thank heaven." Without conscious thought her hand reached out to squeeze his across Tyler's chest.

"What do you say we pack up the baby and head for Liberty Park for what's left of this day?"

Her heart picked up speed. "Where is it?"

"In town. We'll buy dinner there and eat under the trees. There's an aviary. We can take Tyler's baby buggy and walk around. That is if you're not too nauseated."

"I'm okay. Dr. Brown gave me a pill in his office. You have to take them in the morning for them to work. I'd love some fresh air."

"Good. Then let's get ready, shall we?"

It didn't take them long to assemble everything and be off. Because of the intense heat, Diane caught her hair back in a ponytail with a white ribbon. Discovering a drawer full of them in the bedroom, she realized she must have worn it like this many times before.

Afterwards she dressed Tyler in a light green sunsuit, then changed out of her dress into a pair of white shorts and a yellow suntop. When they met outside, she noticed that Cal also wore white shorts matched with a black T-shirt. Both of them had slipped on their Italian sandals.

He didn't say anything, but his eyes spoke for him. They smiled at her over the roof of the car. There was a light in them she'd rarely seen.

Though she had no memory of it, something told her they'd done spur of the moment kinds of things like this before. He acted happy. It wasn't something you could fake. That gray look around his mouth had disappeared. There was an eagerness in his demeanor, as if he were truly looking forward to this outing.

In all honesty, she was excited to be out with her husband. Using Annabelle's parlance, Cal was dropdead handsome. His dark hair and eyes, his wellhoned body acted like a magnet, constantly drawing her attention.

Once they arrived at the forested park, she knew she was the envy of every female around. Men noticed him, too. Cal had an aura of sophistication and authority that commanded attention. The sight of such an attractive man pushing the buggy as they walked along the pathways of the aviary quickened her body so it pulsated with excitement.

For a little while it felt wonderful to put everything out of her mind and simply enjoy this time with her son and husband. She felt alive and never wanted this day to end.

After marveling at the various birdlife and laughing together over an adorable family of quail who marched right across the grass in front of them, Cal bought them corn dogs and ice cream.

They sat on a blanket beneath one of the enormous pines and ate their food. Tyler didn't like being left out. They took turns giving him his bottle. "He has to be the best baby on earth."

Cal nodded. "That's because you're such a wonderful mother."

Her breath caught in her throat. "Thank you, but you need to take credit for your part in his upbringing, as well."

"I'll take it."

His eyes gleamed as he said it before he lay down on his back and pulled Tyler on top of him. "Do you remember *The Rubáiyát of Omar Khayyám?*"

She finished the last of her ice cream and wiped her mouth with a napkin. "You mean, 'a loaf of bread, a jug of wine, and thee?'"

He made a noise in his throat. "He couldn't have been a father yet, otherwise he would have said, a loaf of bread, a jug of wine, a bottle of baby formula and thee."

His comment brought laughter to her lips until she realized how cruel it was that she could remember a line from literature, but not as much as one tiny glimpse of her past life.

"Don't!" Cal admonished. Somehow he could read her mind with uncanny instincts and knew exactly what she was thinking. "Just enjoy this moment with me and don't look back."

He's right, Diana.

"I am enjoying it. More than you know."

"So are we." He lifted Tyler above him and blew on his stomach. The baby smiled and made little sounds every time Cal brought him close.

Diana wouldn't be surprised if that excitement caused Tyler to lose his dinner, but she didn't say anything. The baby knew he was loved. She refused to spoil one single moment of this halcyon time together.

Eventually he put the baby down between them. Diana turned on her side and brushed Tyler's face with a large clover. His little eyelids opened and closed on cue. Then he sneezed. Cal chuckled deep in his throat as they watched the baby's reactions.

Tears squeezed out from beneath her lashes. "He's so trusting, isn't he? So sweet and innocent."

"Totally at our mercy," Cal murmured. His gaze traveled to hers and captured it. "That's exactly how you were when I came to the emergency room after your fall. Like a newborn babe, totally defenseless.

"I've been wanting to say this for a long time, Diana. Let me say it now." A wet sheen glazed his eyes. "You're the most courageous human being I've ever known.

"If I had been in your shoes, I have no idea what I would have done, or how I would have reacted. But I know for a fact I couldn't have handled it with your patience and grace."

She felt this suffocating sensation in her chest.

"Thank you for trusting me enough to help you get this far. I was your husband, yet I felt so helpless you can't possibly imagine."

I saw that helplessness in your eyes, Cal.

"You were wonderful to me and the baby. It was easy to trust you."

"Then I have no right to ask for more than that," he murmured in a thickened tone of voice. "Now that it's getting dark, we'd better gather up our son and head for home."

The abrupt change in the conversation caught her off guard almost as much as the pathos in his comment. *I have no right to ask for more than that.* Those words haunted her all the way across the park.

To get to the parking area they had to pass through the midway. A lot of teenagers stood in line to go on the various concessions.

Cal must have noticed her watching them. "Shall we take a ride on the merry-go-round with Tyler before we leave?"

"That sounds fun."

They parked the buggy, then Cal paid for the tickets and they climbed on. "Which horse do you want?"

Hardly anyone wanted to ride the merry-go-round. They could have their pick. "I'll take the white one."

"Good. That leaves the black stallion next to yours for Tyler and me."

The ride began to move. Her horse started to go up and down. By the time the merry-go-round had gone around once, her vertigo had come back with a vengeance. She knew she was in trouble, but her hands had frozen to the pole.

Cal must have seen the terror on her face. He moved so fast his body became a blur. One moment she was sitting on the horse, in the next instant he'd pulled her off. Only her husband could have managed to walk them to the edge while the ride was still moving and jump off without endangering any of them.

He found the nearest bench and pulled her onto his lap, baby and all. "I'm sorry, sweetheart," he whispered over and over again against the cacophony of sound coming from the garish organ music. "I was enjoying everything too much and forgot about your problem. Forgive me."

His body shook as he rocked them back and forth. Such heartfelt concern for her welfare filled her with fresh wonder over this amazing man she'd been blessed enough to marry.

"I'm all right. Really. It's not nearly as bad as that day you took me home from the hospital. Let's just go."

"Hang on to me." He threw one arm around her waist and drew her tightly against him in what seemed like a possessive gesture. She loved being this close to him. She never wanted to let him go.

You don't have to worry about that, she groaned inwardly as the three of them made their way to the car.

By the time they reached their driveway, the dizziness had passed and she was able to make it inside the house on her own. Cal followed her carrying a sleepy Tyler in his arms.

She kissed his chubby cheek. "He should have a bath before we put him to bed."

"Let's give him one together, shall we?"

The countdown had begun. She could feel it. So could Cal. Tonight would be their last night as a family. He wanted to spin it out as long as she did.

Their baby sensed something special was going on for both parents to play with him at the kitchen sink. He loved his bath. As soon as he felt the warm water lap around his body, he came wide awake and kicked and splashed. Some of it hit her in the eye provoking Cal's laughter, the kind that warmed Diana to her bones.

The baby had done her a favor. Now Cal couldn't tell she was crying. She'd been fighting tears all evening, but refused to give in to them.

By the time they wrapped him in a towel and took him to the nursery, both of them were soaked. Neither cared. The act of tending to Tyler's needs filled them both with indescribable joy.

Cal didn't have to say it. She saw pure love in his eyes as he kissed the baby and talked to him while they dressed him in a shirt and diaper and tucked him in his crib with a blanket.

Tomorrow night another set of parents are going to be putting him to bed instead of you.

They'll be strangers.

She had to swallow a sob so Cal wouldn't hear her.

Would Tyler notice the difference? Would he miss the lullabies she sang to him? Would he miss the silly songs Cal made up that caused her to laugh out loud?

"How about a nightcap?" he whispered as they tiptoed out of the nursery and turned off the light.

Yes. Please. "I'm thirsty. That sounds good." She followed him to the kitchen.

"Do you want cola, or something stronger?"

After a moment's hesitation, "What are you going to have?"

"A beer."

"Then I'll have it, too."

His expression showed surprise.

"Does that mean I hated it?" she teased.

His half-smile did crazy things to her insides. "You could say that."

"What *did* I like?" For some reason she no longer felt afraid to learn about her past.

"A little white wine."

"I remember seeing some in the pantry." Before he could get it, she beat him to it and poured a small amount in a glass. He watched her take a sip.

"My old self had good taste," she quipped before drinking all of it.

His brow quirked. "Your new self drank it too fast."

They both chuckled. Again she had the presentiment that they'd often enjoyed moments like this together.

"Unfortunately Dr. Brown won't let you make a habit of it."

"That's right!" she blurted. "I'm pregnant. I forgot. Maybe it's because I don't remem—"

"That's all right." he broke in gently. "I *do* remember the morning I made you pregnant. It was one of those wonderfully fresh June mornings.''

He took a swallow from the can. ''A certain bird always sang outside our bedroom window at dawn. You could hear our sprinklers going in the yard. Through the skylight you could see lavender fading into blue out in the western sky.

''I had been asleep and I was dreaming that you were kissing me. When I opened my eyes, I realized it was no fantasy. You were giving me a kiss to die for.''

Diana felt a crimson tide flow from her head to her toes.

''We both wanted to get pregnant again, but the doctor had warned us to wait a while, to give your body a chance to recover after the last miscarriage.

''That morning you didn't want to wait any longer and begged me not to use protection.'' He hesitated for a moment. ''Though I knew it wouldn't be wise, you would have to be a man and see the sight I held in my arms to understand why I couldn't say no.

''We enjoyed ourselves so much, neither of us wanted to go to work. But you had made a prior appointment with Roman to get there early and catch up on some important paper work. So I very reluctantly let you escape from me.

''An hour later while I was shaving, I received a call from the hospital. They told me my baby was all right, but my wife was being treated for a head injury from a fall. Could I come over straight away.''

He finished the rest of his beer and tossed the can in the wastebasket.

She put her fingers to her lips, remembering the passionate kiss he'd tried to give her at the hospital. "After the morning we'd shared, no wonder you were so hurt when I pushed you away like that."

The pain she hadn't seen all evening was back in his eyes. "Hurt doesn't quite cover it, Diana. Your accident sent me into shock. I was so selfish, so damn busy reacting to your rejection, I didn't have the empathy I should have had for your memory loss. The doctor warned me you were disoriented, but I couldn't comprehend it.

"As I told you at the park—" His voice grated. "You're the bravest person I've even known. I'm ashamed of the way I behaved in the ER."

"No, Cal! Don't ever say that. Don't even think it. If anyone should apologize, I should be the one. You were my husband. No one could have been kinder or more loving."

"I was a stranger to you. *I still am.*"

She shook her head. "No. That's not true."

"Just promise me one thing, Diana."

She began to tremble. "What is it?"

"That after we're divorced, you'll allow me to take you out again."

What? She fell back against the kitchen counter for support.

"Surely you must sense by now that I'm in love with you. If you want to argue about which Diana I love, I have no way of knowing. At this point the two of you are inseparably intertwined.

"When we said our wedding vows, I had no idea I was getting two wives for the price of one. Whether you like it or not, I don't want to be faithful to one and betray the other. I sure as hell don't have any qualms about committing adultery and sinning with both of you. If I had my way, I'd do it on an hourly basis for the rest of our lives.''

Her sharp gasp pierced the air. The sound seemed to please him.

''Deny it all you want but last night the two of you liked being in my bed. Tonight I happen to know that both of you enjoyed my company. To say anything else would constitute a lie on your part.''

''I wasn't going to lie about it,'' she said quietly because her heart was thundering out of control.

Suddenly she saw him reach for his keys lying on the breakfast table. ''Where are you going?'' she called out in alarm.

''The way I'm feeling right now, you're not safe from me. I'll be back in the morning in time to help you get Tyler ready to go.''

Diana felt like she was in a stupor of some kind. She couldn't think, couldn't move.

''As soon as I leave, set the master switch. If Annabelle has done her job then no one can go or come from the house without your permission.''

In the space of a heartbeat he was out the back door. Within seconds she heard the motor of the Saab. Tyler must have heard it too because he started to cry. He never woke up this time of night.

Could the baby sense that his family was on the verge of falling apart?

CHAPTER TEN

AFTER a long drive up Parley's Canyon where he could battle his demons, Cal went back to Roman's for a sleepless night on their Hide-A-Bed. He waited till seven in the morning, then walked across the street to ring the doorbell of his own house.

Judging by the dark smudges beneath Diana's lusterless green eyes as she opened the front door, she hadn't slept, either. Her hair was still in a ponytail. She wore a robe over her nightgown and carried a fussy, flushed-faced little boy against her shoulder.

Guilt smote him. "How long has he been like this?"

"Since you left."

"Here. Let me take him for a while."

It was no good. Tyler refused to be comforted no matter who held him. Cal could tell he had a fever. "Have you called the doctor?"

"Yes. He said it could be any number of things. I've been giving him medicine to keep his temperature down. We're supposed to force fluids, but he fights the bottle."

"Let me try to give him some juice. You go to bed."

"I couldn't. Whitney indicated that the parents would probably come by for him this morning. He can't go anyplace when he's this sick."

"I'll phone her."

"I already did. She hasn't returned my call."

"She will."

Without looking at him she asked, "Did you spend the night at Roman's?"

He followed her through the house to the nursery. "Yes. I would have come back home around one, but I would have had to phone you to let me in, and I was afraid to wake you and Tyler. If I'd had any idea—"

She shook her head. "Please. No explanation is necessary. At least at Roman's you could sleep."

"You want to bet?"

He didn't know if she heard him or not because the second she put a whimpering Tyler back in his crib, he started crying his lungs out.

Without asking her permission, Cal reached for him and walked him through the nursery to the master bedroom. "Come on, little guy. You and I are going to give your mother some time to herself."

After several attempts to console him, Cal finally plopped the baby facedown across his stomach so Tyler's head and feet stuck out on both sides. Then he started rubbing his sturdy back. Suddenly total quiet reigned.

Cal could feel Diana's presence in the doorway. He turned his head, capturing her tender gaze. "You didn't know I had the magic touch, did you?"

Her eyes grew misty. "Thank heaven you came home when you did. I—I think I'll take a shower and get dressed."

"Go ahead."

"When Whitney phones—"

"I know what to tell her," he interjected in a low voice. *My poor darling wife. Little do you know she's not going to phone. She'll be arriving at our door at nine o'clock with the excuse that John Warren got the times confused and told the people they could come at nine to get Tyler.*

Fifteen minutes went by. The baby slept on. Cal carefully slid him onto the bed, covered him with a sheet, then headed for the bathroom to take a shower, as well.

By the time he emerged with a towel hitched around his waist, he discovered Diana resting next to Tyler on the bed. She'd put on white cotton pants and a cotton top in a beige and white print, one of his favorite outfits on her. She'd brushed her hair till it gleamed pure gold. Her beauty trapped the air in his lungs.

When she heard him open a drawer, she turned her head in his direction. Again he saw color fill her cheeks. "Did Whitney call?" she mouthed the question.

He shook his head.

A tortured look swept over her face before she gave her attention to Tyler once more. Cal took advantage of the moment to get dressed in slacks and a sport shirt.

When he was ready, he reached for her hand. "Come on," he mouthed the words and pulled her to her feet. Together they left the bedroom and headed for the living room.

"I thought we'd better come in here because I

turned off the phone in the bedroom to prevent the baby from being disturbed."

"I'm glad you did that. The poor little thing hasn't had any sleep."

"He'll be fine. Babies are tough. They have to be."

She nodded, then looked at him with those pleading green eyes he adored. "How do you know so much about them?"

"I don't."

"You could have fooled me. No matter what I did last night, he wouldn't quiet down for me."

"He probably had a sick stomach. By the time I got to hold him, the pains had diminished and he'd cried himself out."

"You don't think there's anything seriously wrong with him?"

"No. The doctor didn't either or he would have told you to drive him to emergency."

"That's what he said." She walked around, obviously too restless to sit. "I can't understand why Whitney hasn't phoned. Until Tyler's better, he can't go anywhere."

"Diana— Tyler's going to be all right. The people who are coming for him will know how to take care of him. The arrangements have been made. Don't forget. You're having surgery in the morning. You can't put that off or you'll be placing the baby you're carrying at ris—"

He never finished what he was going to say because the doorbell rang.

Whitney had arrived on the dot as scheduled.

This was it.

If his instincts were wrong this time...

Diana grabbed his arm in a viselike grip. "Who would that be at this time of the morning?"

"I have no idea, but let's find out."

She followed him to the foyer. When he opened the door it was Diana who exclaimed, "Whitney— We thought you were going to call first!"

Whitney's eyes darted to Cal's as they exchanged a private message. "I would have, but John misunderstood and told his clients to meet us here at nine. I decided it would be better to just come as fast as I could to tell you what had happened. I realize you need time to get mentally prepared. Obviously they're not here yet."

"Come in," Cal murmured. His wife was so upset she'd forgotten the basic amenities. It was totally unlike her.

As he hugged Whitney he whispered, "Pray this works."

According to Whitney, John Warren had asked a couple of colleagues in his office to pretend to be the adoptive parents. If this ruse didn't work, then the baby would be driven to the home of a certified foster couple and the divorce would proceed as outlined.

Whitney gave his hand a hard squeeze in response before walking into the living room with her briefcase. She had purposely dressed in a smart navy blazer and skirt, an outfit Whitney called her "attorney" look. It was meant to add authenticity to this momentous occasion which could turn into a nightmare before they were through.

Cal had held out the hope that Diana might have

changed her mind about the divorce before now. But it hadn't happened and they had reached the midnight hour.

Perspiration beaded his forehead as he watched Whitney pull out the legal forms which had to be signed.

They would be legal and binding if Diana didn't break down and call off the divorce.

Somehow he'd thought the miracle would have happened last night, that the proceedings wouldn't have had to go this far.

His life, his love, was slipping away from him with every heartbeat. Like that moment in the ER when she'd told him to go away, he felt utterly helpless. *Terrified.*

The doorbell rang again.

"That will be John. I'll get it." Whitney got up from the chair to let the other man in.

Diana's face looked like paste when Whitney escorted the lean, blond attorney into the living room. They shook hands all around, but Cal observed that his wife kept her hand at her side. Her body had gone rigid.

"My clients are outside in their car. As you can well imagine, they're very excited to meet you and see the baby."

Without preamble Diana blurted in a defensive tone, "He was sick all night. I'm afraid he can't go anywhere."

"Don't worry about that, Mrs. Rawlins," the other man explained in a kindly voice. "This kind of a situation can be a good thing because the new parents have to jump right in and care for the child. It will help them bond faster."

Her facial muscles tautened. "Tyler has already bonded with us."

"I'm sure that's true with all foster parents, but in a short time the baby will come to look at these people as his parents."

"Cal? Can I talk to you for a minute in private?"

"Of course."

He followed her out of the living room to the kitchen. She swung around so quickly her golden hair swished against her shoulders. There was an aggressiveness in her stance reminiscent of the old Diana.

"You can't let them take Tyler."

Oh, Lord. Maybe his prayers were being answered after all.

"Diana— That couple is outside waiting."

"I know. But they can't have him!" Her gorgeous green eyes filled with liquid. "He's *our* baby. I found him." Her voice quivered. "He was meant to live with us his whole life."

Cal took a deep breath. "But that means you'll have to live with me your whole life, too."

She swallowed hard. He could see she was searching for the right words. "I know. A-actually I've been meaning to speak to you about that."

"About what?"

"About the divorce."

"Isn't it what you want?"

"I thought I did, but I—I've changed my mind."

Something broke inside Cal. Before he expired

from happiness he had to contain himself for a little while longer. "Why?"

"I can't really go into it right now. Those people out there are expecting to take our baby away. Please tell Whitney that we're officially adopting Tyler. As for Mr. Warren, he'll have to find another baby for that couple."

She sounded out of breath. "Tell them we're sorry for the great inconvenience, but we're talking about our baby's life here. God guided Tyler's birth mother to us. We're a family. We want to stay a family."

"Amen," he whispered against her lips. "I'll get rid of everybody, then we're going to have a long talk."

"All right." She sniffed. "I can't face anyone right now. I'm going to go check on Tyler."

"Give him a kiss for me, too."

She nodded her head, half laughing, half crying before she flew out of the kitchen.

When she'd gone, Cal strode through the hall to the living room, but he wasn't aware of his feet touching the ground.

Whitney took one look at his face and knew the outcome. She squealed for joy and threw her arms around his neck. "It worked, it worked, it worked! Wait till I tell Gerard. He'll tell Yuri and Yuri will tell Roman and Roman will tell Annabelle and she'll tell Rand, and the whole world will go crazy!"

Cal was already crazy. "I owe you my life, Whitney."

"No you don't. It was my privilege to play cupid."

John Warren stood there with a broad smile on his face. "Whew! Your wife is something else."

"Which one are you talking about?"

While Whitney burst into laughter, the other man looked confused. "Never mind, old son." She hooked her arm through his. "On the way out to our cars, I'll explain it to you."

Diana kept her vigil over Tyler who hadn't made a peep since Cal had gotten him to sleep. By now she thought her husband would have come to find them, but maybe there were some loose ends to tie up before the others could leave.

She hated putting everyone out, but one look at her baby lying on the bed next to her and she knew in her soul she'd done the right thing for Tyler.

His skin felt cool to the touch. Thankful that his fever had gone down, she believed the crisis was over. He might sleep for another couple of hours.

Carefully she slid off the bed, aware that she was hungry. She doubted Cal had eaten breakfast at Roman's. He was probably starving, too.

As she was getting eggs and bacon out of the refrigerator, she felt a strong pair of hands slide onto her shoulders.

"You must have been reading my mind. How can I help?"

His touch felt like fire, setting off explosions inside her body. It was impossible to concentrate.

"Do you want to make the coffee? You know how awful I am at it."

"I do. Just tell me one thing first."

She knew what he was asking.

"If you're afraid to say it," he was reading *her* mind now, "I'll say it for you."

"Cal—" Her voice caught.

"You've fallen in love with me."

It seemed an eternity before she murmured, "You know I have."

"Say it," he begged.

"I think I've wanted to say it for a long time."

"Diana—"

He turned her around to face him. She had no defense against the love shining from those velvety brown eyes.

"I'm in love with you," she cried helplessly. "Madly in love." She lifted her hands to his handsome face. "I don't know how to begin to tell you."

"I do, darling."

He lowered his dark head and his mouth found hers. At the first touch of his lips, sensation after sensation spiraled through her body. She couldn't believe this was really happening.

In her ecstasy she moaned aloud her need. They clung to each other in their desperation to become one flesh.

His kiss the other night was only a prelude to this communion of body and soul. Diana had no idea two people could achieve a level of rapture so intense she was burning alive.

To think she might have let her fears deny them this passion. It was incomprehensible to her now.

"Sweetheart—" he murmured on a ragged breath after devouring her mouth over and over again. "You need to tell me what Dr. Brown said about our making love. You did ask him?''

She was barely coherent. ''Yes, darling. He said that after the surgery we would have to abstain for a few weeks, and then again the last two months of my pregnancy. But in between—''

''Bless that man.''

The next thing she knew he'd picked her up in his arms and carried her out of the kitchen and down the hall to her room. When he'd put her down on the bed, he slid next to her. ''Until our son wakes up, you're all mine.''

''Aren't you worried you're going to be exhausted?'' she teased, burying her face in his neck. ''After all, you'll be making love to both your wives.''

''I'm very much aware of that.'' He grinned wickedly. ''I feel like I did on our first honeymoon. My legs are shaking, my heart is hammering. I'm so excited I'm afraid I might die in your arms.''

''Then you're beginning to have some idea of how I'm feeling.''

''I'm afraid not, darling. I'm afraid you don't have a clue how it has always been with us, but you're going to find out. Just hold on to me and never let go.''

''As if I could. I love you, Cal. I'll love you forever.''

''You said those same words to me on our wedding night. I can see I'm going to find both my wives more than satisfactory. All men should be so lucky.''

''O-oh, I wish Veronica could see me now.''

"*Veronica*— What are you talking about?"

"You know. That hormone-charged brunette in our class who did everything but stand on her head to capture your attention."

He started to chuckle. "I honestly don't remember."

"That's good."

His chuckle turned to rich laughter. "I do believe wife number two has a jealous streak. She has nothing to be worried about. I have a thing for golden blondes with green eyes and long shapely legs."

He could always make her blush.

"Something tells me wife number one was cursed with the same flaw. It comes from being married to a man like you."

"And what kind of a man is that?"

"You're so wonderful," her voice shook with emotion, "it will take a lifetime to tell you."

His eyes burned with desire. "I like the sound of that. I like the taste of you even more. You have no idea how I've ached for my beloved wife. Come here to me, sweetheart."

EPILOGUE

"*COMRADES?*" Gerard took his job as host seriously. "Before the game starts, did I ever tell you the one about Whitney when she went into a hair salon in Grenoble?"

"That's in France, in case you guys didn't know," Yuri chimed in.

"She needed a shampoo and set, and she wanted to impress the locals with her knowledge of the language. So my adorable child-bride opened up her postage-stamp-size dictionary, and said in her best fractured French, '*Bonjour, messieurs. Je voudrais un lavage, s'il vous plait.*'"

Immediately Yuri burst out laughing. Gerard followed suit.

"Translation," Roman broke in with a grin. "We're not all linguists like you two."

"That's why you're not as much fun as your brother," Gerard teased. "All right. I won't keep you in suspense any longer. In case you ever wanted to know, a *lavage* is an enema."

That brought the house down. Or rather Gerard and Whitney's condo.

This was the first party Cal had attended with all his buddies and their wives since the birth of his beautiful baby daughter, Heidi, a month ago. But much as he was enjoying himself, he felt a sense of unease because the women had gone out for the food and hadn't come back yet.

He and Diana had become inseparable in the past year, possibly even closer than before her amnesia because they realized they'd been given a second chance at love.

But some habits died hard. One of them was the lingering fear that when Diana was out of his sight, something might happen to her and he'd lose her. Combined with the fact that they hadn't been able to make love for the last three months, his nerves were more on edge than usual.

"As long as we're telling stories about our brides," Rand interjected, "mine was spying on a supposed invalid for an insurance company whom they didn't believe was incapacitated. But they couldn't prove it. So you know my pocket-rocket."

Despite his preoccupation with his wife, Cal couldn't help but chuckle at Rand's name for Annabelle.

"While Phil, one of the PI's from the office, planted himself close by with a camera, Annabelle crept up behind the woman's wheelchair and pretended to bump into it while she was running. Nothing serious, of course. Just a nudge.

"The woman started screaming and jumped out of the chair as spritely as any twenty-year-old. Phil got everything on video. The insurance company paid her a triple fee."

This time Cal laughed until his sides ached. While everyone was trying to catch their breath Yuri nudged Roman. "Tell them what you pulled on Brittany."

"She'd kill me if she found out I told you guys."

"So what is new, *comradski?*" Gerard's smile was wolfish. Roman started to laugh. Cal knew this one was going to be good.

"This was right after we were married. Brit found out that Yuri used to bug Jeannie's car before they were married so he could hear what she said about him. So she got the idea to bug mine.

"From the mobile unit, Phil accidentally happened to see her plant the bugging device inside my car and told me about it. Naturally I couldn't pass up the opportunity to have a little fun.

"Jeannie happened to be out visiting at the time and agreed to help me make a tape. She disguised her voice and we pretended we were having a mild flirtation. When I got in the car, I put the tape in the deck and let it roll."

"How long before your wife spoke to you again?" This from Rand.

"Well, let's put it this way. She turned on the master switch and this master spy couldn't get in his own house!"

The laughter continued to roll.

Yuri nudged his brother again. "Tell them how you got back in her good graces."

"I convinced her to open the bedroom window and listen to the tape from a recorder I'd brought home from the office. Do you have any idea how stupid I felt standing in my own yard at two o'clock in the morning more or less serenading my wife with that ridiculous thing?"

Cal nodded. "Not as stupid as I felt at one o'clock

in the morning outside my house about nine months ago. What makes this worse is, I *told* Diana to set our master switch, never dreaming the thing would do its job!''

His comment produced more barks of laughter. He eyed Rand. ''Your wife does superb work.''

''She does many things superbly.''

''That's our Annie,'' the guys hooted.

''Ja vol.'' Gerard's voice could be heard over the others.

''Did I just hear Gerard take my name taken in vain?''

''Uh-oh.''

All heads suddenly turned in Annabelle's direction. No one had realized the wives had come back. The smell of Greek food permeated the air. A sense of relief washed over Cal. He jumped up from the sofa, needing to be with Diana.

Diana was in the kitchen waiting...

It seemed like she'd been waiting for this night forever. She had special plans for them, and was so excited she was trembling.

Whitney had arranged this get-together to throw Cal off the track. Brittany's dear friend, Denise, had agreed to tend Heidi and Tyler until noon tomorrow. Everything was set. All Diana needed was her husband.

To her delight she didn't have to seek him out. He entered the kitchen like a man on a mission. Just knowing he was in the same room with her sent delicious chills through her body. She stayed by the sink sipping some water.

His arms slipped beneath her parka to hug her waist. "Welcome back, my love." He moved her hair aside and kissed her neck in a certain sensitive spot. "Don't you want me to help you off with this?"

"No, I think I'll keep it on."

After a quiet pause, "Where's our food?"

"I thought we'd have something different than Greek tonight."

"Why?"

"You'll find out. Let's go." She grabbed his hand and started pulling him toward the back door.

"Sweetheart? What are you doing?"

"We're going to get our dinner. Come on."

"Does Whitney know about this?"

"Everyone knows."

At this point he was not only intrigued, he was starting to get excited as he followed her out in the snow to the parking lot.

"I'm driving. Don't worry. We're not going very far."

True to her word, they only had to travel a couple of miles before he realized they'd passed through the gates of La Caille, a French restaurant located on a piece of wooded property with a vineyard near the road to Alta Canyon.

To his shock, before they reached the manor house itself, she made a right turn off the winding drive to reach a little snow-covered cottage tucked in the trees. Though he'd never been inside, he knew this to be a favorite honeymoon spot for newlyweds.

Lord. His heart started to pound too fast.

"Come with me." Her smile melted his insides.

He got out of the car and followed her up the steps on legs of mush. When she opened the door, a facsimile of a French hunting lodge greeted his vision along with the hidden amenities of modern civilization.

A fire had been lit. Shadows from the flames leaped as high as the dark wood beams and danced on the walls. An elaborate candlelit dinner awaited them, complete with a magnum of champagne.

He shut the door before pulling Diana back into his arms. His emotions were overflowing. "I thought Dr. Brown told us we had to wait six weeks."

"He lied. Happy Valentine's Day, darling."

Diana's face glowed from an inner light. Her eyes, her hair, everything gleamed green and gold fire. The freezing night air had put roses in her cheeks. Her mouth...

He groaned before capturing it with his own. Their kiss went on and on. Her lips, her hands, her body overwhelmed him with all she wanted to tell him, all that was in her heart. He never wanted this ecstasy to stop.

"You've done everything for me. Everything!" she cried with an ache in her voice. "Whitney finally admitted to me what you did to make me call off the divorce. Thank God you understood me better than I understood myself.

"Now it's my turn to do everything for you. Tonight I'm going to wait on my magnificent husband. I plan to adore you all night long, starting now." She kissed his chin. "Stay there and don't move."

Cal couldn't have moved if he'd wanted to. Diana had created this night for the two of them. This manifestation of her love thrilled his heart to its very core.

As he drank in the atmosphere, she walked back in the room wearing a white toweling robe that reached her knees. Over her arm lay the same robe for him.

With her feet bare, her hair a floating cloud of gold about her shoulders, she resembled an angel.

No words passed their lips, but their eyes communicated their love as she slowly undressed him and helped him into his robe. After tying it at the waist, she led him to the pillows in front of the fire. When he was seated, she knelt in front of him, poured them both some champagne and handed him his glass.

She raised hers in the air. Her luminous green eyes gazed up into his. "To heaven. It's wherever you are."

Cal's body trembled as she intertwined their arms. They began to kiss between sips, anticipating the rest of the night to come. Each kiss grew deeper, longer. Cal savored the intimacy of this moment as a gift only Diana had the power to give him.

Her sweetness, the beauty of her body and soul acted like a drug on his senses. The measure of his entrancement was so great, he scarcely realized she'd put her glass down and had taken his right hand in hers.

"With this ring, I thee wed for now and all eternity."

His heart slammed into his ribs as she slid the simple antique gold band home.

"As you can see, it's not like the one I put on your other hand. That ring is shiny gold, inlaid with diamonds. That one represents all the hope of a bright new love. Of beginnings.

"This one—" She pressed his hand. "This one represents true passion, constancy, fidelity, loyalty. Enduring love.

"Together the rings represent perfect love. That's the gift you've given me. It's a priceless treasure I'll never take for granted.

"I love you, Cal. I love you."

There were no words. Cal leaned down and gathered his bride to his heart.

In 1999 in Harlequin Romance® marriage is top of the agenda!

Get ready for a great new series by some of our most popular authors, bringing romance to the workplace! This series features gorgeous heroes and lively heroines who discover that mixing business with pleasure can lead to anything...even matrimony!

Books in this series are:

January 1999
Agenda: Attraction! by Jessica Steele
February 1999
Boardroom Proposal by Margaret Way
March 1999
Temporary Engagement by Jessica Hart
April 1999
Beauty and the Boss by Lucy Gordon
May 1999
The Boss and the Baby by Leigh Michaels

From boardroom...to bride and groom!

Available wherever Harlequin books are sold.

HRMTB

If you enjoyed what you just read,
then we've got an offer you can't resist!

Take 2 bestselling
love stories FREE!
Plus get a FREE surprise gift!

Clip this page and mail it to Harlequin Reader Service®

IN U.S.A.	IN CANADA
3010 Walden Ave.	P.O. Box 609
P.O. Box 1867	Fort Erie, Ontario
Buffalo, N.Y. 14240-1867	L2A 5X3

YES! Please send me 2 free Harlequin Romance® novels and my free surprise gift. Then send me 4 brand-new novels every month, which I will receive months before they're available in stores. In the U.S.A., bill me at the bargain price of $2.90 plus 25¢ delivery per book and applicable sales tax, if any*. In Canada, bill me at the bargain price of $3.34 plus 25¢ delivery per book and applicable taxes**. That's the complete price and a savings of over 10% off the cover prices—what a great deal! I understand that accepting the 2 free books and gift places me under no obligation ever to buy any books. I can always return a shipment and cancel at any time. Even if I never buy another book from Harlequin, the 2 free books and gift are mine to keep forever. So why not take us up on our invitation. You'll be glad you did!

116 HEN CNEP
316 HEN CNEQ

Name	(PLEASE PRINT)	
Address	Apt.#	
City	State/Prov.	Zip/Postal Code

* Terms and prices subject to change without notice. Sales tax applicable in N.Y.
** Canadian residents will be charged applicable provincial taxes and GST.
  All orders subject to approval. Offer limited to one per household.
  ® are registered trademarks of Harlequin Enterprises Limited.

HROM99   ©1998 Harlequin Enterprises Limited

Strong, seductive and eligible!

THE AUSTRALIANS

Stories of romance Australian-style, guaranteed to fulfill that sense of adventure!

This June 1999, look for

Simply Irresistible
by Miranda Lee

Ross Everton was the sexiest single guy the Outback had to offer! Vivien Roberts thought she was a streetwise Sydney girl. Neither would forget their one night together—Vivien was expecting Ross's baby. But irresistible sexual attraction was one thing...being married quite another!

The Wonder from Down Under: where spirited women win the hearts of Australia's most independent men!

Available June 1999
at your favorite retail outlet.

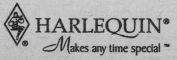

HARLEQUIN®
Makes any time special ™

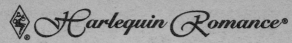
Harlequin Romance®

We're proud to announce the "birth" of a brand-
new series full of babies, bachelors and happy-
ever-afters: *Daddy Boom.* Meet gorgeous heroes
who are about to discover that there's a first time
for everything—even fatherhood!

We'll be bringing you one deliciously cute
Daddy Boom title every other month in 1999.
Books in this series are:

Who says bachelors and babies don't mix?

Available wherever Harlequin books are sold.

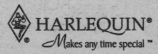
HARLEQUIN®
Makes any time special ™

Look us up on-line at: http://www.romance.net

HRDB1-R

Harlequin Romance®
Coming Next Month

#3555 THE BOSS AND THE PLAIN JAYNE BRIDE
Heather MacAllister

Jayne Nelson feels her life lacks pizzazz. She's just spent her twenty-eighth birthday working overtime for her accounting firm. Then Garrett Charles walks into her life. Talk about pizzazz! Though Jayne realizes he's out of her league, that doesn't stop her daydreams becoming X-rated! But Jayne wants more than dreams…

#3556 TO CLAIM A WIFE Susan Fox

Caitlin Bodine is the black sheep of her family—and Reno Duvall certainly blames her for his brother's death. For five years, he's cut her out of his life. Now he's forced to share his ranch with this beautiful, heartless woman. He doesn't like it one bit, and neither does Caitlin! Only, living together, they discover how they've misjudged each other. Reno wasn't looking for a wife, but he becomes determined to claim Caitlin for his own…

Rebel Brides: *Two rebellious cousins—and the men who tame them!*

Meet Caitlin and Maddie: two beautiful, spirited cousins seeking to overcome family secrets and betrayal. As they come to terms with past tragedy, their proud, rebellious hearts are tamed by two powerful ranchers who won't take no for an answer!

Look out in July for **To Tame a Bride.**

#3557 THE PARENT TRAP Ruth Jean Dale

Matt Reynolds finds Laura Gilliam infuriating—and the feeling is more than mutual. Unfortunately, their kids have decided that they'd make a perfect match! But though Matt realizes that his little girl needs a mother and Laura that her little boy needs a dad, they're determined not to fall into the parent trap! But is it too late?

#3558 FALLING FOR JACK Trisha David

Jack Morgan has been left to bring up his small daughter Maddy single-handedly. It wasn't easy. Then Bryony Lester fell into their lives. Maddy warmed to her instantly—how could Jack resist a woman who could make Maddy smile?

Daddy Boom: *Who says babies and bachelors don't mix?*